Pastorale

ILLINOIS SHORT FICTION

Crossings by Stephen Minot
A Season for Unnatural Causes by Philip F. O'Connor
Curving Road by John Stewart
Such Waltzing Was Not Easy by Gordon Weaver

Rolling All the Time by James Ballard
Love in the Winter by Daniel Curley
To Byzantium by Andrew Fetler
Small Moments by Nancy Huddleston Packer

One More River by Lester Goldberg
The Tennis Player by Kent Nelson
A Horse of Another Color by Carolyn Osborn
The Pleasures of Manhood by Robley Wilson, Jr.

The New World by Russell Banks
The Actes and Monuments by John William Corrington
Virginia Reels by William Hoffman
Up Where I Used to Live by Max Schott

The Return of Service by Jonathan Baumbach
On the Edge of the Desert by Gladys Swan
Surviving Adverse Seasons by Barry Targan
The Gasoline Wars by Jean Thompson

Desirable Aliens by John Bovey
Naming Things by H.E. Francis
Transports and Disgraces by Robert Henson
The Calling by Mary Gray Hughes

Into the Wind by Robert Henderson
Breaking and Entering by Peter Makuck
The Four Corners of the House by Abraham Rothberg
Ladies Who Knit for a Living by Anthony E. Stockanes

Pastorale by Susan Engberg
Home Fires by David Long
Canyons of Grace by Levi S. Peterson
Babaru by B.Wongar

PASTORALE

Stories by
Susan Engberg

UNIVERSITY OF ILLINOIS PRESS

Urbana   Chicago   London

For Charles, Siri, and Gillian

*Publication of this work was supported in part
by grants from the National Endowment for the Arts
and the Illinois Arts Council, a state agency.*

"Lambs of God," *Kenyon Review* 30, no. 120, issue 3 (1968); reprinted in
Prize Stories: The O. Henry Awards (1969)

"Pastorale," *Sewanee Review* 84, no. 3 (July/September 1976); reprinted in
Prize Stories: The O. Henry Awards (1978)

"Small Voices," *Southern Review* 14, no. 1 (Winter 1978)

"In the Land of Plenty," *Iowa Review* 10, no. 2 (Spring 1979); reprinted in
The Pushcart Prize, VI (1981–82)

"Trio," *Massachusetts Review* 21, no. 4 (Winter 1980)

"The Lap of Peace," *Kenyon Review* 4, no. 1 (Winter 1982)

"The Face of the Deep," *Sewanee Review* 89, no. 3 (Summer 1981)

Library of Congress Cataloging in Publication Data

Engberg, Susan, 1940-
    Pastorale: stories.

    (Illinois short fiction)
    Contents: Lambs of God—Pastorale—Small voices—[etc.]
    I. Title.   II. Series.
PS3555.N387P3   813'.54   82-4730
ISBN   0-252-00993-2   AACR2
ISBN   0-252-00994-0 (pbk.)

Contents

Lambs of God

Everything was coming to life, Helene said. Did the girls see how green the willows were? She pointed to a watery fissure between mounded fields. If Leonard wouldn't drive so fast—she looked sidelong past little George to her husband—they would all enjoy the scenery more. She lowered her sewing to her knees and winced as the car plunged down a hill and dipped up to the next rise. It wasn't even pleasant driving that way, she said. Why was he in such a hurry? Why couldn't he just relax and enjoy the trip? They were only going down to the farm, after all.

Sixty was a good speed, he said. Didn't she want to get there before dark?

Not if it meant making everyone sick and missing all the spring sights besides. The new lambs were out, and the baby pigs, she said. It was important for the children to see all that. There, look. Had they missed it? They had passed a pungent-smelling barnyard turned to choppy brown sea by the footprints of animals. In the muck had been sows weighted down in their own eating by suckling farrows. She sighed. The burdens were great; sometimes it seemed to her that she was fighting all alone, that to her only it now seemed unbearable, altogether wrong that they should be going sixty miles an hour through Iowa farm land which at no other time of day, at no other time of year would look exactly this way—opened by the plow, misted by the evening, gauzed in hollows and on distant ridges by palest green. Had they seen it? Baba? Sarah?

Sarah pressed into her corner of the back seat, her head against the jolting window, and tried to protect her trance-like abstraction of wires and flying telephone poles from the intolerable bombardment of her mother's words. She put up a finger, the better to upset rows of birds along the swooping wires, and left the encumbrance of answering on Baba, whose duty it was anyway, being the eldest. Yes, said Baba, she had seen it. But she was so miserable, she added: her eyes watered, her nose itched; couldn't anything be done for her?

Sarah only pressed harder to the window when her sister's body, slumping fretfully against the seat, gave in to its restless discomfort, and mother said, poor Baba.

Sarah must close up her window—right away, said mother. Poor Baba. Where on earth had she gotten these allergies? All from his father, no doubt, she said to daddy; and Sarah envisioned the red face of grandpa and the way he would look that night, standing with grandma on the yellow-lighted back porch of the farm house to welcome their arrival.

"All that hurry was for nothing then," said mother; for it was already so dark as they lurched up the lane past the garden that the car lights threw beams on swarms of insects while daddy stopped to open the wide white gate, and as the car curved around the pump house, the startled eyes of cats glowed and vanished in the unfathomable dark spaces beneath the slatted corncrib. They were waiting on the porch as Sarah had imagined them; grandpa came forward; the engine was shut off. It was necessary now to rouse herself and carry in the picnic basket, the empty egg crate, to accept a kiss from grandpa's stubbled cheek, an embrace against grandma's pillowed bosom. She shivered from a sense of open space and unlit night beyond their small illumined circle, out there space vast enough, or so it seemed to her, shivering, her arm crooked inside the old wooden egg crate, to surround the farm with the entire dome of moon and stars.

"No, you're going right upstairs to bed," said mother to little George. "You'll have time for all that tomorrow."

"Here, my fine friend," said daddy, lugging his son beneath one arm to the hand pump beside the stoop, "we'll give you one squirt," and Sarah, hearing the wheeze and clank of the straining pump, remembered her old joy in the gushing water, so that she shouted, urgently, for the water had not yet rounded the crook, "I will—let me," while she dropped the basket and the loose-jointed crate and ran to put her full weight on the clammy handle that brought out the first rush of brown water into George's hands. Again and again she threw herself on the handle until mother's voice was saying, "All right, all right! Leonard, you've let them get all wet."

Beneath the nursery window as she fell asleep she heard the soft bells of sheep, and her hand beside her face was perfumed with the earthbound scent of iron rust.

Sarah woke in the night to the wind, throwing itself against the loose nursery windows. In its troughs of quiet she heard the chime of a clock from some lower hollow of the drafty house and the sonorous push and pull of heavy people sleeping: she was at the farm. The room had its own smell. She lay high up on the hard, humped bed, exposed to the air, to the dark spaces around the radiator, to the light that seemed to come from inside the vanity mirror itself. On the ceiling the circle of stars and moons and animals still faintly glowed. Grandpa had put them up for George. They were magic, he said. She stared until she wasn't even sure she saw them any more.

The windows rattled, and a glide of white passed through the doorway and took the shape of mother over George's bed. Then the form came to her; she saw a limp bit of ribbon at a nightgown's neck.

"Mom?"

"Sarah, are you awake?"

"Where are the sheep?"

"The sheep? Somewhere safe, I'm sure. Did the wind wake you up?"

"Where is Baba sleeping?"

"In with grandma. Are you warm enough?" Mother tucked the covers around her face, and Sarah felt eased into a cave of muffled sound.

"Then where is grandpa?"

"He's in his own room, of course. Now you must go back to sleep. Are you warm enough?"

"When does the clock go?"

"Did you hear it just now? In another fifteen minutes it will strike three times for three o'clock. But you'll be asleep by then," said mother.

"Why are you up?"

"Well, you know I don't sleep too well when daddy snores. But someone has to get up to cover you children. Why, if I didn't, our George-boy would sleep all night without a single cover on." Mother stood up.

"Do I need covering?"

"There now, you're sleepy. Do you hear how sleepy you sound?" Sarah listened, and she heard the wind. An extra blanket, smelling like the closets, was pulled up.

"Mom, put the lights on once more so the stars shine. Please."

"It will wake George."

"Please."

"All right. Close your eyes." Sarah felt the body coming closer and the lips touching her forehead. Then she was alone; beyond her eyes the light flared a moment and was gone, and the voice whispered from the doorway, "Now. Open."

She opened her eyes and saw shining animals swimming in space; especially she stared at a round moon within a ring that grandpa said was a planet. "Good night," said the voice. The new blanket was tucked all around her ears. And though she waited for another chime, trying to keep her eyes on the glowing circle above, she didn't hear again the clock that would still go off every fifteen minutes, even in the middle of the night.

Finally it was morning. All night, it seemed to Helene, she had been fitfully riding the tops of waves, barely sleeping, until a moment ago when the first bird calls washed her up to solid wakeful-

ness. It was a relief to see light at the lace curtains, to smell the op-
timistic freshness that separated morning from night air. Early
morning: this was her time; it had been ever since the end of those
drugged, slow-motion days of early marriage when the very atmosphere in which she moved seemed to have been formed of thick
fluids. The difference had come gradually, a slow recovery from the
shock of discovering herself a woman. A little common sense ap-
plied here and there, and she had managed to emerge from those
persistent waters. She stretched in the old double bed beside heavily
breathing Leonard and began exercising her feet, pointing her toes
in a rhythmic, rolling motion. Well, for one thing, she knew a great
deal more about the simple facts of health than she ever had as a
young woman—decent breakfasts, enough milk and protein and exercise, sensible shoes and coats. She knew that when she was tired,
she must either sleep or eat something nourishing and that when her
eyes began to smart with the difficulty, the sadness of what could
happen to people, even beyond the cause of their follies, she must
set her mind on doing something practical and generous and near at
hand. Rolling and stretching her feet one last time, she felt the
muscles tighten all the way up her legs.

It hadn't been easy, teaching herself all these lessons. She had
never had a mother to do what she was doing for her daughters, and
she had had to come around to most things by herself. There had
been people, of course; all along the way there had been dear people. She sighed. Some of them were even dead now: Mrs. Knack
who had boarded her as a young teacher and who had embroidered
and edged with handmade lace three sets of pillowcases for her small
dowry; Professor White who had said for her to put away his busy-
work and run along to the lecture, a fine girl like her; Vera Bell,
taken so soon, a real painter, who had said she would give anything
for a fresh complexion and strength of mind like hers. She sighed
again. And then there was her father.

She sat up abruptly and let her bare feet down to the stiff wool
guest-room carpet. At least she had learned enough to get out of bed
when she woke and not waste these peaceful hours. She moved
quietly around the room with her dressing, at which she had trained
herself to be quick, knowing from experience what a waste of time it

was, what a giving in to emotional backwaters, to ponder oneself in front of a mirror. The maddening thing was how difficult it had become lately to put herself together properly. So often now her stomach felt heavy and bloated, her feet ached, and her hair seemed stiff and unmanageable. She hooked her stockings and straightened up in front of the old vanity mirror. Behind her in the dim light was the heavy walnut bed, draped at the foot with the white bedspread and filled in the center with the mound of Leonard's body, which could sleep in such exhausted weight and dampness, could be so insistent, so masculine, and was so quietly aging. As was hers.

She lowered her eyes and pressed her lips together. There were some magazines with articles on education in her basket downstairs; she could begin those while she had her coffee. George had spilled food all over his sweater in the car last night; she must wash that out. And the bathrooms, she had noticed, smelled of urine; she must find some disinfectant and see if she could, without grandma's knowing it, get those toilets cleaned: they simply weren't safe for the children this way. She hung up her night clothes and took a last look around the room. Sunrise was close.

Downstairs she pulled up the dining-room window shades. The sun would come in directly there, in the window by the drooping fern plant overlooking the barnyard with its walnut tree, grassy cistern mound, and red and white buildings. The rising sun would fall upon the far sides of the buildings, it would warm her face and touch the oak wall paneling behind her. She turned. Halfway up the wall, where the paneling stopped, a shelf supported a row of decorated plates and mugs. In the center of the room was the heavy table, covered with a green cloth. By the big window was the magazine table and the rocking chair with the handwoven rag mat that she admired, in the corner the tall clock that she seemed to have heard each time it struck the night before, and beside her the divan of rough wool where her father-in-law slept after each meal, turned on his side toward the wall, his wide overall straps crossing over his back, his fringe of white hair damp and curly over his red ears, and his deplorably enormous stomach hugged like a watermelon in the curve of his body.

She saw the body as it would lie there; it turned, it rattled in its throat, it slept face up. How little did grandma and grandpa know of her, yet over the years had she not proved herself, shown that she, too, was thrifty and hardworking, in touch with the plain and the sorrowful? How could one help but learn these pains? How could one help but be overcome, subdued, saddened when glimpsing the burdened sow, hearing of a couple who had lost both their children in some freakish way, watching the mask of illness take over the face of a friend? Hard forces waited for everyone; hard forces made one humble.

Yet it was her great talent, her great mission, she told herself as she crossed decisively to the kitchen to make herself coffee and oatmeal, that she could imagine the largest effects from the smallest acts. It was a sense of history, that's what it was; the sense of her place in the historic line of Christ's servants was a disquieting nimbus around her that would not let her say, "It makes no difference." And so she had opinions—how could she help it, when she saw some child stumbling in the dark of dumbness, all because no one had ever taken the trouble to talk to him. Or when some stupid ox of a man was let into some position of authority, all because—well, sometimes she wasn't quite sure why such things happened.

By the time she had settled herself at the kitchen table with the steaming bowl and cup, the sun had risen, reflecting red in some windows, gold in others. It was very nice to be eating good oatmeal with the sun in the room like that; if the rest of them could only see her, they would know how indestructible she was, how alert, how far above the ordinary run of women. Grandpa would be coming down soon for the chores, but for the moment she was quite alone, as solitary as she had been as a girl at the lake or as a young teacher living in an upstairs room of someone else's house. But of course she had hardly known what to do with herself then, so ignorant she had been, ignorant and foolish; sometimes late at night when she would sit in the big chair under the light with her head tipped back, her eyes closed, her book fallen, she had to press her lips together and shake her head at how much she had had to learn. She wished all those people from her past could see her, then they would know that she wasn't so foolish as to go through life untouched, that she con-tinually gathered her energies together and did what she could. The great duty was to take a stand, to accept the terrible burdens, to survive the imperfections. Her mission, her talent was to make everything count, to put meaning into everything she did.

In a jagged flash she remembered her eldest daughter. The morning light faltered when she saw again the slender body, the heavy, falling hair, the stained underclothes as she had seen them last night in the hollow, drafty bathroom. Too fast, things sometimes seemed to be going too fast now, so that she didn't know what to do with them; parts of herself were left behind, part of herself still stood at the basin while the water turned red and Baba shivered behind her.

It wouldn't be so difficult if only she could slow down their life; she must set her mind now on keeping it in hand. Leonard, for example, had been working entirely too hard. Why, it shocked her how battered he seemed sometimes, and yet he didn't seem to know what was happening. Did he even realize that he hardly ever read a single word that didn't have to do with his blessed business? Turning on the lamp in the alcove by the table, she crossed her legs and opened the magazine. If she thought about these things too much, she'd never get anything done.

One by one she turned the pages. The children were too young now, but some day they would understand what her world had been, what she had fought against, what she had been given to work with. Some day they would marvel at her energy and her wisdom, and because never, never had she been indifferent to them, they would also excuse her for mistakes she had never known. And didn't everyone need excusing? She excused grandpa, she excused Leonard, she forgave the spring for coming so inevitably, so sadly around again.

At the photograph of a lined, pensive face she stopped. It was the face of a famous French sculptor and beside the picture was an interview. She read quickly down the page. He ate his breakfasts of coffee and hard rolls in a restaurant not far from his studio: an egg or two would do him better, she thought, and he was smoking, too. No, he answered the interviewer, he had never changed his lodgings; he had, in fact, found himself working in a smaller and smaller space in his modest studio, never feeling the need to surround himself with possessions: she raised an eyebrow; it was curious that he could work with his hands and still not have a healthy respect for the objects of life; she herself knew what it meant to have a satisfactory teapot and the right silver tray for squares of soft, fruity cake. She turned the page to see photographs of his statues. A neverending, lifelong search, the editorial caption said, for the essence of man. Of course, what was wonderful about these magazines was that they brought you up close to things you'd never see otherwise. The same with television. Why, she heard lectures and interviews there that put her in touch with the whole world. She took a sip of coffee, and it was deliciously fragrant and warm. In a moment she would get up and start being useful. She finished the last of her oatmeal. Here she was eating her breakfast and looking at the studio of a famous sculptor.

In the corner of the page was a picture of the artist's wife in a loose, untailored dress, and beside her a row of figures for which she had been the model. The sculpted breasts seemed to hang directly from the sinews of the neck. Well, it certainly would be strange having a husband like that and sitting naked in front of him all day. She wondered if this were his first wife, but the caption didn't say. A never-ending, lifelong search: she looked up from the magazine to the gleaming stove, the glass cracker jar, the cross-stitched sampler on the wall. It would be something, all right, to be married to someone so wrapped up in a single purpose: with a man like that she might have been a much different person. She would have lived in Paris; she would have met such a different lot of people. And it was the people one met, she was firmly convinced, that made all the difference. Think how far she had come since she had left home. And yet sometimes she felt that she had never met quite the right people; somehow no one understood quite what she might have done. Again she looked at the picture of the sculptor's wife. It was very possible, of course, that this poor woman did nothing but pose for her husband all day, cook his food, make his bed and lie in it with him, all necessary and worthy duties, but perhaps she slouched about unkempt; perhaps neither of them cared a bit about the education of their children. Now, what Leonard had was a love of solid, basic things; that was what had appealed to her, the idea of being a good

wife to a solid man, of making herself a positive force against discomfort and disorder and sorrow. For of what good was her mind,
she had asked herself in those early days, until she had first tied
herself to the solid, basic things? One shouldn't stay untouched; one
shouldn't be too proud. And what she had already learned about life
was more real than anything these artists, or those questionable psy-
chologists, for instance, could discover. One didn't know anything
about life until the children came, and the sorrows, and the
sacrifices, and the terribly difficult times.

From upstairs she heard the creaking of a metal bed and the long
wheezing coughs that meant grandpa was getting up for the chores.
She patted back her hair and took another sip of coffee. Maybe it
would be better if he found her at work. She rinsed her dishes at the
sink by the wide kitchen window overlooking the orchard, made up
some nice rich suds in a basin, and began washing out George's little
sweater. Apple trees, in full bloom, spread like layers of lace down
the sloping orchard. The wind was still up, she saw; in the pasture
valley the cottonwoods sustained one slanted, shivering pose after
another. He would be down soon. She worked at the spotted
sweater. One step at a time he was coming, in a labored, arthritic
tread, his low groans mingling with those of the wooden banister
that bore his tremendous weight with each of his downward lunges.
She sighed, she pressed her lips together. The morning was coming
on too quickly. Grandpa lumbered so painfully down.

"Good morning, grandad," she said in her brightest, most practical voice as he came wheezing into the kitchen.

He unlocked the back door, opened the screen, and spat into the
yard.

"I've made some oatmeal," she said. "You'll have some, won't
you?" She saw with horror that he was wearing no underpants
beneath his loose-fitting overalls, for at their side openings his white
flesh showed smooth and round and promised to plunge to an abyss
beneath the stomach that he was forced to heave along with each
rocking, stiff-legged step.

"Oatmeal? Nah, no oatmeal." He was putting on a denim
jacket and an engineer's cap. His taciturnity, familiar as it was to
her by now, still set off eddies of uneasiness around her, especially

in the early morning with only the two of them in the kitchen that was usually staged with the squat figure of grandma at the spotless sink. Sometimes it seemed to her that he would die, and he would never know any more about her than he did now. But he loved the grandchildren; that she knew. She had given him the only grandchildren he would ever have, and thinking this, she said brightly, "But of course you're going to have something to eat. Can I fix you an egg?"

"I'll wait," he said and went down the steps and the walk and through the gate into the barnyard. She watched as he went first to the windmill to turn on the pump; then he disappeared, and she knew he was urinating on the far side of the tool house. At the corn-crib he disappeared again and a few moments later emerged with two buckets of corn. "Shee-eep, shee-eep, shee-eep," she heard him call. "Shee-eep, shee-eep, shee-eep." Leaning on the pasture gate, he threw the ears one at a time. The sheep came in a wave over the crest of the hill, nodding, running as if they were one amorphous animal. She watched until he had thrown all the corn, and then she turned back to the kitchen.

When Sarah woke, she heard bells, one alone, two never quite together, perhaps more, and kneeling at the low, dark wood window-sill, she saw that there were indeed three black-faced sheep almost directly beneath her at the drinking trough by the orchard fence. Now and then a head was raised, a pink mouth opened, for a jerking bleat. She put out a hand to touch the light curtains that puffed out and sank back with the wind. The air that surrounded her had been over the numberless fields, through the blooming orchard, and like the trees, she shivered in the vast breezes. Below her the sheep moved slowly and absently; absently, softly she stroked the filmy curtain.

At breakfast grandpa said he had a surprise for the girls, but mother said Sarah couldn't leave the table until she had eaten some protein. "You simply can't go out in that wind with nothing but sweets in your stomach. I won't have you girls eating only cookies and waffles."

"Won't hurt 'em," said grandpa, who poured thick sorghum from a white crockery pitcher into the hollows of his waffle. The light from the big window gleamed on his bald head.

"Grandpa, tell us the surprise," said Baba. Her heavy blond hair was clipped neatly back on one side, and Sarah saw that she was sitting up very straight and eating her boiled egg. The night before Baba had had some secret with mother in the bathroom, and this morning, too, she had locked the door and told Sarah through the fuzzy, patterned glass to wait a few minutes. "Tell us what it is," she was saying, but in a grown up voice.

Taking George up on his lap, daddy tried to get the boy to finish his egg and oatmeal, but Sarah saw that he cleaned up the bowls himself.

"Leonard, won't he eat?" asked mother.

"Slick as a whistle," said daddy, holding up an empty bowl and winking at Sarah beside him.

"It won't be no surprise if he tells you," grandma was saying to Baba. Her voice sounded high and tight, what mother called strained. "Those waffles are made with eggs," she said to mother.

Sarah took a mouthful of egg and then another. Breakfast seemed to have been going on for a long time. Beyond grandpa's molded head a green dust sifted from the trees; across the fields she could see deep brown and yellow-green and brown and green in endless rolls and strips; a black and white and yellow spotted cat stopped before the low window and lay down at the edge of the walk under the green, sifting dust. Somewhere upstairs a door slammed, and the glass fringe on the lamp by the rocking chair tinkled with sounds that weren't even notes. Mother was saying something to grandma about being anemic and white in the face and tired, and Sarah saw that the small, pouched face of grandma at the end of the table was very white. She probably needed iron was mother's opinion.

"How are the thistles, dad?" asked daddy, still playing games with George, who leaned far back against his arm and looked at Sarah upside down.

"You want to salt 'em down?"

"And the orchard needs clearing, too. Come on, my fine friend," he said to George. "Up you go. We've got work to do."

Helene put up a hand to protest: Leonard toted the boy so rakishly under his arm. "Leonard, he has just eaten." George's laughter rippled, was sucked in, and gushed forth in uncontrollable delight. But the next moment the boy was on his own two feet in the kitchen, and so she relaxed her arm, took a sip of coffee, and said instead, "He's had a cold, you know. You'll have to watch him every minute to see that he keeps his ears covered."

The girls, too, would have to wear scarves, she said, as she stacked up dishes. These spring winds could be so dangerous. And then she looked at Baba, her eldest girl, because she had felt again the jagged memory, and she said, "And you should keep absolutely warm all over today, do you hear? Try not to get a bit chilled."

"Why? Why shouldn't she?" Sarah heard her own voice almost shouting out.

"Because. That's why," said mother, and her voice sounded tired; it lingered wearily after her as she carried the dishes to the kitchen.

Kittens were the surprise. "Oh-h," Sarah stooped down in the dusty summer kitchen to the rag-filled box, "how old are they? I want the yellow one."

"They ain't very old." Grandpa stood in the doorway. "A week maybe. We've been keepin' 'em for you."

Daddy lifted George down from his shoulders. The kittens lay in a silky heap beside their long black mother. They were all different colors, like the discarded bits of cloth in the box.

"Why don't they move?" asked Sarah. They lay so still she was afraid they were dead.

"Go ahead. Pick one up," said grandpa.

But of course she had played with kittens before; she knew how to pick them up. You pinched a little fold of fur at the back of their necks and dangled them up through the air to your arms. They liked it because that was the way their own mother carried them. She reached into the box and pinched up a fold of fur. The kitten dangled in the air, it curved itself up like someone poked in the middle, it opened its mouth. Then she had swung it up to cradle it under her chin and all was safe. Her fingers twitched with how easy it had been to pluck up the scrawny living bit and swing it up through the air. She reached down and took up another one and held them close to her cheek. They squirmed and curled delightfully, and she could manage them both very well in her hands.

"I want," fussed George until he was told to sit on the cracked cement floor and a kitten was put in his lap. Baba took hers to the rocking chair. There were six kittens in all. The black cat sat up stiffly, and Sarah saw that her stomach was white.

"Does she mind?" she asked. The black cat seemed to blink directly at her through slits of eyes.

"You go ahead," said grandpa. "I saved 'em for you."

"I'm taking mine for a walk," she said and slipped around grandpa's stomach into the sun, ducked under the dish towels snapping on the line, and came out at the front of the farm house, never used as an entry, where a half-finished sidewalk from the white porch ended in spongy lawn beneath the mulberry trees. With each step she sank down upon the burrows of moles that crossed beneath the trees like humped veins; with each step she saw ceilings of tunnels crashing to floors. Well, it couldn't be helped: she had to walk, but sometimes she did follow deliberately the crest of a tunnel, making sure that she had leveled it neatly down. The moles were a nuisance. Grandma had said so.

"Hey, stop it," she cried as a kitten wriggled from her grasp and clawed its way across her shoulders. She ripped him from her neck. "Naughty cat. Bad cat." She shook him in her hand. It was so easy; he weighed almost nothing. She shook him again, and he panted soundlessly through his pink mouth. "Naughty cat," she said, but less fiercely, while she zipped down her jacket and made a warm pocket for the kittens in the crook of her arm. It would have been easy to clamp her arms over them and press hard until they could no longer breathe; they were about the size of two furry tennis balls, only soft—bellies as soft as pulpy fruits.

"We'll go to the barn now," she said, "and then I'll take you back to your mother." She peered into the jacket and saw that they were lying one on top of the other, very still. Sometimes tremors passed from the kittens into her own arm and side.

She turned down the driveway through the wide gate into the

barnyard, past the corncrib where she breathed the half-musty, half-fresh odor of the million tumbled cobs. Beneath the crib, between its high, piled stone foundations, was the home of all the cats, an uneven bed of dirt and rock whose innermost shadows were never touched by light. Kneeling, she saw not a single cat, yet imagined she heard them. "This is where you'll live," she said into her jacket, but the kittens seemed asleep. She jostled them, but they only nosed more deeply against each other. Funny little things, they might have been sleeping safe against their mother, the way they looked. She wondered if they were hungry.

She took them to the barn, through the lower half of the heavy side door, over the high, worn stone sill, up into the dim room where stiff and dusty harnesses hung along the wall and the small panes of the windows were crusted with dirt and cobwebs. The barn was formed of so many stalls and separate rooms and rafters and hayracks sticking up like slanted fences that there were places where she had never been—rooms behind rough doors whose wooden latches she could not turn, stalls separated from her by insurmountable partitions beyond which she could only hear muffled thuds of animals enclosed. Even now, as she stood, holding the kittens tightly, her shoes already deep in the smelly straw, she saw the cap of grandpa appear on the far side of a room through dust and stripes of sun and disappear as a door opened and closed. "Grandpa!" she called, but he must not have heard. She waded past a row of stalls to a door that she could open by lifting a peg. Surely he would be there. She sat on the sill and slid down into the hay of the two-story, center section of the barn that ran like a cavernous avenue between the two enormous doors she had seen opened only once, to let a hay wagon in. "Grandpa?" A pigeon flew high among the rafters with a brushing sound, settling far back over a loft. The kittens were making noises now, urgent peeps. "Okay," she said, "wait a few minutes and then I'll take you back."

"Grandpa?" she said, but all the high, cupboard-like doors along the wooden avenue were closed. Surely a door would open, and he would come out. From the spaces above her a shaft of sun fell through swirling straw dust to her feet. "Grandpa?" she called out again, but she heard only the bleat of a sheep. The wagon doors strained against their heavy bars and a sudden shower of straw fell loosely from the loft for no reason. Whirling around, she saw nothing behind her, and then she could not be quick enough in climbing back up through the door and straining toward the sunny opening that framed a warm brown field and far away the rises and dips of the yellow road.

The light in the barnyard dizzied her with its brightness. She need-ed to go to the bathroom and to wash away the taint of breakfast syrup from her mouth. "Shut up," she said to the kittens in her jacket. "Quit it," she almost shouted, for they were curling their claws into her side. What was going wrong? She shuddered to remember the obscurity of those interior spaces, the way she had glimpsed in secret the back of grandpa's cap as he worked, the mysterious whirr of birds in the far reaches of the lofts. Running as if the shadow of the great building were at her heels, she came at last to the familiar cistern mound, her place, to whose grassy top she could climb in the same way the sheep did, by a long gangplank of heavy boards. Here she was high enough to command the whole yard; from here the barn looked as it always did, and she might never have been inside, hearing her own voice as it died in the dusty silence. She sank down and let the kittens into the grass. Yes, here, certainly, she was safe. There was the back door of the house, where she had come from breakfast, where she would go for lunch. Con-tinually, absently, she turned the groping kittens like mechanical toys from the perilous edge of the cistern. She would forget about the barn.

Anyway, she had done nothing wrong, for she was allowed in there. Seeing grandpa that way, though, made her feel alone and strange with herself. It was like the time she had glimpsed him tink-ling on the tool shed, or when she had come upon mother crying in the bathroom, or when they had gone over to the other farm, which was rented out to the family with all the children, and she had seen in the barn the terrible metal milking machines, making noises like grandma's old washing machine, hitched up to the soft, round cows. She hadn't been able to tell anyone how she had stared at those pumping cups; still in her mind the sex of the animals wavered between the warm female of milk and the hard male of the enslaved teats.

Stupid little silly kittens. They had no idea where they were. Grabbing them up abruptly, she lolled back and dandled them above her chest. She dropped one to the forest of grass and before it could recover its balance, snatched it up again. A slow, hot shiver convulsed her as she let them both fall and watched as they righted themselves and sniffed toward each other. Above her, in a new tack of the wind, the half-dead branches of the walnut tree scraped and clacked upon each other. She saw daddy squatting far down in the pasture with George, and for a moment grandpa in his overalls appeared at a barn door to throw water from a bucket, an explosion of drops in the wind, after which he looked up at the sky and lurched back into the black interior. Inside the hollows of her body she felt vaguely sick.

She stood with the kittens and began to walk around and around the top of the cistern; the orchard and summer kitchen and walnut tree and house and garden and tool shed and barn circled around her in the opposite direction. The ground under her was strewn with dead branches and stones and sheep droppings and a rusty metal wheel with a wide rim. She shook the kittens in front of her face. "Where are you going, sillies, where are you going?" Very badly now she needed to go to the bathroom. It was the barnyard that whirled around them. And before she knew it, she had dropped a kitten to the base of the cistern; she had held it out like that by the scruff of the neck and just let go. She let go of the second kitten, and then her hands were empty. Further down than she could jump the kittens crawled toward each other. She stood watching them, chewing hard on the end of one of her braids, until a door slammed at the house and she looked up and saw mother in someone else's old jacket and a bunched-up scarf over her head, her hand shading her eyes, walk toward the pasture where daddy stooped, killing thistle roots with spoons of salt, Sarah knew, for she had once followed behind, throwing the coarse grains into holes left by the spade.

What had happened? It was still morning, only closer to noon; mother pushed through the gate; the towels still flapped by the summer kitchen. And before it should be too late, she clambered half-crouching down the same rough planks and followed the damp bands of metal that encircled the cistern wall to the place where the kittens still stumbled near each other. She bent over them. They were all right then. Cats had nine lives, grandma had said. Hunkering down, her chin on her knees, she pondered on the eight remaining lives of the kittens who seemed too soft to be crawling in the coarse rubble of the barnyard, and she pinched them up to her arm gently and with remorse, for she had not meant to be the one to take away their first lives.

Gently, her head bent protectively over them, she carried them to the summer kitchen, out of the wind, and with a shudder of relief let them down beside the black cat, who stretched up from the mass of rags and nursing kittens and bobbed her head again and again over the returned babies, licking their eyes, their heads, the hollows between their forelegs and stomachs. A fly droned against a window, and near her feet Sarah saw a black spider, its legs groping over a crack in the cement. Never once did the black cat cease her rhythmic caresses.

The noon dinner seemed quite satisfactory to Helene, and everyone ate well, except that grandpa put far too much grape jelly on his cottage cheese. There was beef that had cooked with onions over a low heat all morning, potatoes peeled and mashed with cream and butter by grandpa himself, applesauce and sweet watermelon pickles put up by grandma, a good mess of last year's asparagus from the freezer, cottage cheese and milk and bread and butter and jelly, and for dessert strawberries unthawed to cool sweetness and cookies stuffed with dates. She kept George beside her, settled nicely on a chair with a farm catalogue under him, and saw to it that he got down all his meat and potatoes before he was allowed more applesauce. Everyone seemed sleepy, and Leonard and the girls had new, high color in their cheeks from the wind. In fact, Leonard looked exceedingly well; his gray hair was blown up from his forehead, so different from the flat style he wore to the office, and though he ate noisily and with bent concentration, she didn't mind for once. He was relaxed; he helped Sarah to more applesauce; he told his father that he'd build a bonfire in the orchard, that the thistles would be done in an hour or so, that the sheep looked good, very good—would he want to do the shearing while they were there? She watched him sweep a piece of bread around his plate for the last of the gravy. Projects—those were what Leonard loved: getting a bit of garden in shape, stripping the paint from some old chair, clearing an orchard of dead wood. Sometimes it seemed to her that he should never have left the farm, that the way they lived now left him no freedom.

"Mo' ap'sauce," begged George, but she said, wiping his cheeks, that he had had enough, he'd get the gollywobbles if he had any more, that he must finish his milk.

"You like grandma's applesauce, don't you?" said grandma in the special tone of voice she always adopted for the children.

"We all do," said Helene. "Did you use the Wealthies for it?"

"There's all different kinds in there," said grandma. "The apples was all good last year."

After lunch grandpa slept even before the dishes were done so that Helene had to tiptoe through the dining room past the couch where he was stretched and whisper to the girls reading magazines in the darkened front sitting room that they should go up to their beds for half an hour. Daddy and George were already upstairs; grandma had just gone up. They must be very quiet. And she? Well, she was going to rest downstairs, for daddy was sure to be snoring. Now off they must go. She was too tired to argue.

But they protested. They hadn't had a nap for years. What was she thinking of? All they were doing was reading magazines, which was restful anyhow, and there they would stay.

"You at least should sleep," she said to Baba, for they were sprawled on the couch where she herself had wanted to nap. "Your body needs extra rest right now. How do you feel?"

"Achy," said Baba, looking up, "in my back and my legs. My nose itches."

There now, she might win her daughter over. "It's sleep you need," she said quickly. "Some day you girls will have to learn how to take care of yourselves." But it was no use; Baba plumped herself

more deeply into the couch, and Sarah rested a flushed cheek
against a crocheted tidy. "I'm too tired to stand here and argue,"
she said. "Only don't come to me at suppertime and say you're
too sleepy to set the table or help clean up. You both left all
the work to grandma and me this noon, and that's fine because you
were out of doors enjoying yourselves, but it can't be that way all
the time; it's too much of a strain on grandma. But I won't argue
with you." She left them with a sigh she couldn't control: it was so
difficult for her to get enough rest these days; her family was
spreading out around her, scarcely leaving her enough peace of
mind for her own needs. Wrapping herself in a heavy tweed coat,
she sighed again. All through her dishwashing her tiredness had
grown until she had become impatient listening to grandma and had
told Leonard that if he didn't take charge of George for a while, she
wouldn't be able to get through the day. She gathered up her sewing
and basket of magazines and took herself through the dining
room— quietly, for grandpa groaned and turned in his sleep—out
to the porch swing where she sat down on the stiff wood, her hand
on the chains that supported it, and gazed out at the long veranda, at
the trees constantly in motion and full of the sound of the wind and
the soundless drifting of blossom dust, at the cut in the land where
the road ran, and at the distant farms distinguishable by barn roofs
and clumps of trees. She closed her eyes and let herself be carried
with the swing. Already she had been up over eight hours, and there
were eight more to go before she could rest again. It was so terribly
difficult to get enough sleep: if it wasn't someone's sickness, or
Leonard's snoring, or her own racing mind and aching muscles,
then it would be one of the girls, off on some adventure with her
friends, or Leonard, up in that tiny company airplane, doing more
business than any man should be asked to do; with all that going on
she simply couldn't get her own rest. She kept her eyes closed and
rested her head on the back of the swing. There had been a swing on
the house her father built; for long hours as a child she had rocked
there, watching the fruit trees and grape vines and vegetable garden
dip and rise before her, probably because, she was able to reason
now, she had once been told that her mother had often sat there with
her father in the evenings. They had been great talkers, an aunt had

told her; they talked so much the neighbors wondered how they found so much to say to each other.

She saw them, suspended together from the porch roof, her mother pregnant, her father dressed in his jerkin, his measuring stick still folded in his pocket perhaps; she saw them through a neighbor's window—it was before she had been born—through the fruit trees and the pillars of the porch. But she couldn't hear what they were saying. She stopped the swaying of the swing with her foot.

And if she herself were to be seen right now? Straightening up, she turned her coat collar against the wind, tucked her skirt tightly around her knees and picked up her sewing. Some of the people in the distant farms knew who she was, would recognize her if they drove by just now, for she had spoken to them at birthday parties or funeral dinners; they must think of her as the clever wife Leonard had found at the university. Would they think it strange that she should sit here spending so much time on a little handiwork? That was what amazed people, even her own friends: her contradictions, how she could give a lecture, or talk with ease to the most important sort of people and still put out a roast-beef and apple-pie dinner that satisfied even nameless hungers, or know exactly how to appreciate the most common people, or raise three children such as hers, who so far had brought her nothing but credit, being healthy and quick at school and already singled out by her friends and the teachers for special talents. It was hard for people to put all this together. Why, one time after she had spoken to a group of parents at the grade school, a man had come up to her and said right out that he thought her the most remarkable woman in town. After that she had gone home in such a flush that she had put up eight quarts of applesauce before going to bed.

The only trouble was that sometimes things seemed to be getting out of control. She found herself objecting quite irrationally to Leonard or the children, not being able to stop herself. But of course she herself worked just as hard as Leonard, and it was true that if anything went wrong, if they got sick, for instance, all the trouble would fall back on her; she'd be the one to sit up at night and clean up the bathroom messes and cook the special food. Yet it frightened her sometimes the way her voice would suddenly come out, objecting, as if the reasons for her speech were far down, out of reach. Sometimes it seemed as if she had lost hold on her life, as if at some imperceptible point she had been dispersed irretrievably into the people around her.

She rocked in the swing, barely moving, and made stitches so neat and small they were almost invisible. In the midst of this wind, these wild dartings of cats across the lawn, these uncontrollable movements of animals—a sheep had gone into labor, grandpa said at noon—and of the family within the house—George would have kicked off his blankets by now, and Leonard, snoring, would never know—she glided tightly in place, one foot on the wooden porch floor, her fingers looping stitch after stitch through the yellow binding and the printed cotton. Her face felt drawn with weariness. It was so terribly difficult to make a day turn out right. She pressed her lips together and looped a series of perfect stitches.

"Sarah, do you know what's going on in this picture?" Sarah looked. Her mouth felt raw from sucking hard candies, and her whole body burned with exhaustion and excitement, for she had been reading of what people called Nazis had done to naked prisoners in cold rooms with showers and cement floors. She looked at the picture and saw two heads, a man's and a woman's, and a hand with painted fingernails pressing into flesh. "Well, do you know what's going on?" demanded Baba.

"What is?"

"If you don't know, I'm not going to tell you. Give me back the book," said Baba. "Now. Look at this one."

She looked and saw huge rocks around which stood naked, decorated Negro women with big bellies and children at their legs. "It must be in Africa," she said. "Whose is that?"

"It's a book of photographs daddy sent for. Those women are going to have babies—see? And they've all been sent up there to the rocks together."

"Why?"

"To have them, of course."

"Don't they have hospitals?"

"This is in Africa. Come on, let me finish it first," said Baba urgently and took back the book. Her hair hung down one side of her face, and she was chewing on her barette and snuffling. There was a pile of candy wrappers on the coffee table that they would have to hide later from mother. Sarah went back to her magazine.

"After insertion, the glass tubing was broken," she read, "making urination an excruciating process." The row of cows, the gleaming milking machines took places in the cold room with the cement floors. Her teeth felt as if they were rotting in her mouth; daddy had said cavities could start in five minutes. "Baba, what did you do with your kitten?" she asked.

"Put him back, naturally. Mother said mine had fleas all over it. Did yours?"

"I don't know," she almost whispered.

"The day we leave they'll all get killed, you know."

"Killed?"

"Drowned. In a bucket. Grandpa always does it that way."

"That isn't so."

"Ask and see."

"How do you know?"

"I found out."

Sarah unwrapped another candy and pressed it hard against the roof of her mouth until it was crushed and the soft center oozed out. She heard grandpa get up from the couch in the next room. "Ah!" he cried out sharply, "ah!" as he rose to his feet. She held the shattered candy shell firmly with her tongue so that it almost hurt and stared at a patch of sun on the dark flowered carpet until the sweetness had dissolved. Candies went quickly; the best moment was just before the centers broke out. Again her mouth felt raw and empty. She imagined shattered bits of glass within flesh in a cold room, within the cows' drooping teats which the big boy with the red face had enclosed so deftly with the metal cups. Cats had waited in the straw and muck. "They always comes around at milkin' time," the boy had said. "They sure is smart."

Throwing down the magazine, she stretched herself taut and then crumpled into the couch. How long would it take to eat every candy in the bowl? Idly she counted as many of them in their metallic wrappers as she could see. The wool sofa pricked right through her shirt.

"I think I'll go outside and look at the kittens," she said aloud, but continued to lie immobile in the stuffy room with the sun shining around the lowered shades. In her mind she was unwrapping another candy and holding it, round, uncrushed, on her tongue. It would have been better if she hadn't done that to those kittens. Every time she remembered with vague disbelief what her hands had done, how they had just let go, she wished it could be undone. She hadn't meant it at all; she had just been going round and round the cistern mound.

"I guess I'll go outside," she said again.

Baba blew her nose and lay back sighing. "Sarah, don't tell mother that I showed you that picture."

"Which one?"

"The first one."

Sarah saw painted fingernails digging into someone's skin. She thought of them all the time that she was washing her own hands and brushing her teeth hard in the bathroom by the kitchen. She saw them again as she stood over the box in the summer kitchen watching the kittens pressing their paws into the black cat while they nursed. Her two kittens were there with the rest. She stooped, but she didn't touch them. "I'm sorry," she whispered. The big black cat stared straight ahead with half-closed eyes. A heavy flying bug snarled against a window. "I'm sorry, kittens," she said again, but not a single kitten turned away from his eating. What she had done was secret, then; even the mother cat didn't know that her kittens had fallen. Easing up so quietly she thought as she stood at the door she could still hear their faint slurps of nursing, she slipped outside.

So bright was the sun that she could barely open her eyes to the blooming orchard and the white dish towels twisting from the line. All the swift, fresh morning shadows had given way to droning air and fierce sun, which she felt sink into her hair and neck and back as she settled herself cross-legged on the hitching stone, facing the broad, afternoon facade of the barn, and began twisting her fingers, painfully, repeatedly, into the metal hitching ring. She smelled manure and blossoms and the metal fence behind her and the rotting walnuts on the ground. The long grass on top of the cistern was like someone's hair, ruffled up; she thought she could see the flattened down place where she had sat with the kittens. That had been before lunch, when the sun had still come from the other side of the barn, and grandpa had stepped out of the shadowed doorway to throw water from a bucket. She twisted her fingers again and again through the metal ring.

When she next looked up, grandpa was coming toward her from the barn, rocking from side to side, holding something in his arms, passing the corncrib and then crossing the gravel drive, coming straight toward her and, she saw now, carrying in his arms a lamb, all four of its legs thrust down.

"Here," he said. "Sit still and hold him." He put the lamb into her lap. "Put your arm over him. Hold him tight. Hold his front legs tight." Then he went on through the gate to the house and left her with the wriggling, curly-haired baby lamb, who looked right up into her face and bleated, "Mehh, mehh," with a catch in the sound. His tongue was as pink as her own. She felt his fluttering heart in the round, firm chest she cupped in her hand and saw that his hair was rough and kinky even over the bones of his head and down between his eyes. "Meh-h," he bleated and pushed his nose hard up against her cheek and into her ear and along her neck. "Ah!" she cried and bent down to hold him close as he nosed back to the warm place on her neck where the sun sank into her braids.

"Here," said grandpa. "Give him this." He put a bottle with a long brown nipple in her hand, and she could feel that the milk inside was warm. "You'll have to push it in. Hold it up. He ain't used to this."

Grandpa held the lamb's head while she pushed the nipple through the black lips. Milk dribbled down his woolly throat. "Give him a minute. There he goes," said grandpa, as the lamb suddenly pushed against the bottle so that she had to hold it firmly as he sucked and the wool along his throat rippled with the milk going down inside.

"Is he sick?" she asked.

"Nah, he's just got a ornery mother. Won't feed him. They do that sometimes. Won't have nothing to do with their own babies—

maybe a wrong smell.'' Grandpa took his hands from the sheep. ''You like that?'' he asked. He was wheezing heavily, in through his mouth, out through his nose with his lips pursed. When he opened his mouth, she could see all the gold caps along his teeth.

''Yes,'' she said, looking back at the lamb standing tensely on her lap, his whole body straining up to the bottle, only his short tail and his lips and throat moving.

''You can have him then,'' said grandpa.

''You mean I can take him around with me?''

''You got to feed him.''

The lamb drank two bottles of milk right there, and she had to jump up suddenly while he tinkled all over the stone block.

''Haw, haw,'' said grandpa. ''Did he get you wet?'' He was feeling the lamb all over with his big hands. He looked into his mouth and ears and eyes and felt along his throat and legs and belly with hands that seemed to know what they were feeling for. ''There ain't nothing the matter with him. Do you want to take him with you?''

''Anywhere I want? Grandpa, anywhere I want?'' she had to repeat, for he had already turned away and was frowning in the direction of the barn. Still not answering, he heaved himself to his feet, steadied himself, and started off across the yard. It was as if he had forgotten her and the lamb and everything that had happened. Grandpa was funny, like the way he turned his back on the dining room when he slept on the couch, the way he could go right to sleep, even with people still at the the table. ''It's all right,'' she said softly to the lamb, and the sound of her voice talking to him was strange. She would have to go some place very quiet where she could talk to him.

''Meh-h,'' bleated the lamb sleepily as she carried him through the orchard, past the first rows of trees and down a slope until the house behind them was almost hidden. After they were settled in the grass, she loosened one of her hands and then the other, but he didn't run away; he stood stiff-legged beside her, his black nose twitching in the wind, and she noticed with awe that his eyes were fringed with the finest pale lashes. Talking to a lamb was not as easy as talking to a kitten. It made her feel as she sometimes did sitting on the edge of her bed in front of the mirror and pretending that she was two people, that she was herself and that she was also someone else who didn't know herself. It was as if he might be able to understand what she was saying, the way he looked at her and the way he stood so separately beside her.

She touched the high, flat hump of his head, then slipped her arm around his body, wondering if he were seeing what she did: the two rows of dark pine trees at the bottom of the orchard, the cotton-woods in the valley of the sheep pasture, the sunny fields beyond that looked as if the cupped palm of a hand had firmed them up the way one made hills in moist sand. She looked as far as she could see, and it seemed as if she had never tried to see so far; it seemed as if she had never seen how trees looked ten farms away, how the clouds piled close to the ground in the distance and burned moving shadows across the fields. "Hello, sheep," she said, stroking his back; he ducked his head up again and again under her caressing hand. She wasn't hurting him; she was being good to him. "Lamb, I dropped some kittens," she whispered suddenly, but he only ducked his head up again to receive her touch. If she were to stroke him long enough, in the right way, it wouldn't make any difference about the kittens. "Anyway, I think they're all right," she said close to his ear. He pushed his nose along her neck and she could feel his breath and the curls of wool under his chin.

Never had an afternoon been more beautiful. "Isn't it beautiful?" she said to him, and it seemed as if she had never used the word before.

When she heard voices higher up in the orchard, she crept down the hill with the lamb to the pines where the light descended sharply into dusk. She had never been here alone before. Damp brown needles covered her shoes with each sliding step. All sound was sub-dued by the dense branches. She crouched at the base of a tree and from beneath the lowest shaggy branches saw again the sunlit fields; almost near enough for her to touch ran a fence and a field with plowed up chunks of earth sliced sharply down their sides as if with a knife. She looked at the slim, paired pine needles at her feet and then at the sliced sides of earth and then out to the horizon again, this time almost level with her eyes. The kittens were all right; they had forgotten everything. She would eat no more candy. Every day she would feed the lamb and bring him down here. "Don't worry," she said to the lamb, who sprawled across her lap. Leaning back, she felt how her braids got caught in the flaky bark of the odorous tree.

Helene paused, her hand still on the banister. For what had she come up the stairs? Sunlight wavered through the rough bathroom glass as if through water; late sunlight flooded from the open nursery door across the old hall carpet. Something from the nursery? She smoothed a patchwork quilt at a bed's corner. Something for George to wear? Brilliantly dappled sunlight slanted through the mulberry trees, and she heard shouts from the orchard where they all were working now, where she was going in a moment, but first having come upstairs for something, something. No, not for George: she had seen him off, bundled him up herself, made him promise not to loosen his scarf. Something for someone. "You go ahead. I'll be out in a minute," she had said at the back door, straightening up from helping George, knowing from the feel of the skin on her cheeks how tired she was. She had forced her legs to climb up the dark stairwell. She had come up into the airy hall, the bedroom doors open around it, the broad, loose windows shaking from thudding gusts of wind, sunlight streaming from the west. Now she was wandering—into the bathroom reeking of asparagus urine; into grandpa's undecorated room where the metal clock ticked loudly on the marble dresser; into grandma's room with its half-drawn shades, the Bible by the bed, the glass case of Leonard's early books. She tapped the case before the books—all stories of success, rags to riches, and guides to self-improvement. Was it something for grandma? It was disgraceful to have forgotten so easily, to have come all the way up those stairs for nothing. Leonard had taken George piggyback to the orchard.

Yes, it was for Leonard. She stood in the doorway of the guest room. It was the camera, and it had been her idea, too. "We must have a picture of this," she had said as she saw even grandma dressing for the wind in a faded purple scarf and a lumpy jacket. And George had been so fresh from his nap. She tucked the leather case under her arm and touched on fresh lipstick at the mirror. "At the farm. May. From left to right Grandpa, Grandma, Helene, George at four years, Baba, Sarah.'' Already as she descended the stairs she was labeling the photograph, filing it; already as she put on her own coat and walked down to the orchard she was seeing her great-great-grandchildren finger the picture in some future living room. Helene, the mother of those children, the wife of that man; Helene, the intelligent one in the tweed coat; Helene, holding that little boy by the hand. She pushed open the gate. The sun was just right for a photograph.

But they had already started the bonfire; it crackled and snapped in dangerously high flames, and—she stopped dead—there was George all alone fiercely throwing sticks at the fire's edge. As she began running she could see piles of branches already gathered here and there among the trees, and as she finally reached her son Leonard was coming up along the fence, dragging half a tree behind him. ''Leonard!'' She heard her own voice, high-pitched, frantic. Indignation collected as she watched him come laboriously into earshot, but she couldn't help herself: there was no excuse for what he had done; it made her so weary to think of it. He stopped before her and let his branches crash to the ground. He was exhilarated, she could tell. ''Leonard, what, what were you thinking of when you left George up here alone by the fire?''

''Why, he's all right. What are you fussing about?''

''All right! A child that age is never all right near a fire without supervision. What were you thinking of?''

''I thought he'd be all right.''

Her husband's hands looked awkwardly empty at his sides, but she couldn't stop herself. ''What am I to think when you do something like this?'' She felt only the weariness of her life. A flame burst near her, and a falling branch sent up a spray of sparks. George was tearing twigs from the wood Leonard had dragged up.

''Look at me,'' he said to them, and he threw the twigs hard down into the fire.

Still she couldn't stop. ''When anything happens to one of them, I'm the one who does the worrying. You're not home enough. You have no idea how difficult it is for me when they're sick or hurt.'' She felt her eyes smarting from the difficulty of her position, from the outrageous thing Leonard had done in leaving a little boy alone by a fire. And in a wind, too. There was no way out but to keep on talking and talking. A flock of birds crossed above them in a dense, whirring fan.

Leonard interrupted her. "He's all right, Helene. He's just been running back and forth. I've had my eye on him."

The sun was coming straight at them now, through the trees. She pressed her lips together. "Well, I won't say any more, but you should have known. Are you still going to take this picture? The sun is going." He reached out for the leather case. She saw his hand, stubby and hard, reaching out from the leather sleeve of his jacket. It didn't seem to belong in the same place with the sound of her voice; it shamed her. She watched the hand tilt a light meter this way and that in front of her face. Beyond was the sun and against it she saw grandma and Baba, coming up the slope with their arms full of sticks and then grandpa, rocking slowly behind them, dragging branches.

The hand folded to the precision of the camera. She closed her eyes and stood with the sun on her face. She would have liked to stand so still that the parts of her life came home to her in a single luminosity; she would have liked for the sun to burn into her until she was loosened to the bone, made ready, as once she had been, to the feel of the touch of hands.

"Leonard, you have taken so many nice pictures," she murmured, opening her eyes, but her husband was no longer near her; he was crouched on the far side of the fire with George. Her throat tightened with the loss of her life.

And yet there was nothing, really, that she didn't have. No, of course there wasn't. Here they all were—her children, her husband, the irreplaceable older generation that gave such ballast to their lives. Everything was fine. This was just what happened. And who after all would judge them in the end? One never knew what history would make of them. She straightened her collar. She was an extraordinary woman; that she must remember and then go about setting her mind on doing what she could. This photograph, for instance: wasn't it so typical of her, so admirable, to understand how important such a document would be for the future? Of course it was.

And this trip: wouldn't it make a difference, one way or another, that the children had been driven at dusk through the spring country, in the wake of the plows and the dark nights of animal births?

"All set," said Leonard, leading George around the edge of the fire.

"Are we all here?" she asked. "Where's Sarah? Baba, come here and let me straighten your hair. Daddy wants to take a picture. Grandma. Grandpa. George, don't run away. Where shall we stand, Leonard?"

She clipped back Baba's hair. Already her daughter was taller than she. "You should have a scarf on," she said. "Does anyone know where Sarah is? Leonard, can you whistle?"

"Why, don't this look nice?" said grandma. "Leonard, I want you to make me a copy if it turns out."

Sarah was still crouched under the pine tree when she heard the whistle. For a long time she had been waiting for the lamb to finish sleeping. A chill, like a layer of colder water beneath the sunstruck surface, had settled among the trees so that she turned up her collar and burrowed her hands into her sleeves. Then for a brief time a golden slant of light had transformed the floor of drab needles into radiant copper until a rise in the field finally blocked the last of the sun. Her cheeks felt as if she had been running in water. It was important to stay absolutely still, to let the lamb sleep, to watch the light slant in and disappear as it would. Every time she remembered the kittens, the sick, rich aftertaste of the candy, the naked prisoners in rooms colder than milking stalls, she held herself even more deliberately so that nothing should now be spoiled. Yes, never had an afternoon been more beautiful. This was what could happen.

"Wee-oo." The whistle came in two tones, higher, lower.

"Wee-oo. Sar-rah."

"Now we can go," she said to the lamb. When she stood, there was nothing around her but the black-green grove. With the lamb under her arm, his heart thudding in her palm, she stooped beneath the branches one last time to see the place where she had been—the fence, the plowed earth heaved up so close to her that she might have been a creature living in its ridges, the fields of color beyond running up the world until they merged into the sky that arced overhead and landed someplace, always behind her.

"Sar-rah."

"Coming," she said softly, as the lamb nuzzled in the crook of her arm, and now there was nothing strange in the sound of her own voice as it was let loose among the branches.

As she carried the lamb up the hill through the blooming trees, she could see uncurling licks of flame and smoke and then the whole fire, consuming into pure molten color the disorderly heap of dead branches. The fire was beautiful. Everyone was standing in a row beside it. Mother held George by the hand. "Wee-oo," whistled her father, waving his arm, while behind him the fire crashed down into its center and sparks gushed up as high as the house. She began to run. "Wee-oo."

Pastorale

There was a woman who for a time loved a younger man. Her name was Catherine, and she had lost a child. Her daughter had been in a coma one week, two weeks, and then one morning in October her expression had changed slightly and she had died. Hanna. She had had honey-colored hair and pale eyes with an outer rim of darker blue to the irises. Until the brain tumor she had been healthy enough and lively and competent. She had bought two goats with her own money, raised them up, rode with John to have them bred, and when they freshened, milked them herself, morning and night, and with part of the milk made yogurt for the family. Catherine took over the milking. The boys should be doing that, John said, but she wanted it for herself; the goats, at any rate, were almost dry.

She was forty; Hanna had been ten. Sometimes the rounded numbers rose up in her mind as a meaningless chant—ten, twenty, thirty, forty—and then she would look backward and forward and see nothing but inexpressive decades. Her own face, resting against the goat's fur above the stream of milk, felt used up, like a land-scape of dry runnels. She cleaned the stall methodically, accepting everything—the smells of urine and dung, the impatience of the goats, the cold in her hands as she fetched the water—as she had begun to accept the death itself.

But beneath this methodical impassive continuance of life, she could feel her grief changing into something less bearable than the immediate anguish; it was a sense of absolute physical loss, of strange yearning: she wanted to touch the child again. There had been no chance to be alone with her, dead. At night Catherine would lie in the dark and think that she might be all right if only she could cradle the child's actual corpse one more time.

But of course that was impossible. Months were passing. The adolescent energy of their two boys continued on a course of its own, as if it had been a stream of water passing through the house and out again, seldom anything to hold on to, and she had the feeling that wherever they were going, they were already on their way. Childhood had never seemed to her so brief.

She and John were the maintainers. In the past they had occasionally joked to each other, companionably, about how they were merely the keepers of an establishment. A door would slam somewhere, there would be a thumping on the stairs, a call from the barnyard, and when they looked at each other, what was between them had to do with seventeen years of marriage and the pleasure they could still take in each other and the way these people who were their children had invaded their house, but only for a time. Now between them Catherine sensed a self-consciousness that it seemed discussing would only aggravate, and although they might be alone, she no longer felt the same privacy. She would lie in bed, watching him undress, and the sight of his bare back, twisting to pick up a shoe in the half-light, or of his hair and beard—how grizzled he had become!—made her want to cry out to break through this theatrical intimacy, but the sound remained voiceless. He seemed to have become gentler with her, sometimes distant. They talked, of course, and they had wept together and with Tom and Drew, and they both had their work, which was a blessing.

John had been having good success with his pottery; he would be showing at two large invitationals that early summer in addition to the usual regional exhibits, and he was working steadily now, seldom sleeping late in the morning, seldom coming in early from the shop to read or tinker with an odd repair. She herself was finishing up one commission from the nursing school, the illustrations for a handbook for expectant mothers, and on the strength of this had been given another by a biology professor, an essay on reproduction intended for high school and college students. The coincidence between these subjects and Hanna's death she endured, because of her desire for work; she was practical and energetic by nature, and she had always handled periods of unclarity or doubt simply by applying herself to what was at hand. Several times a month she drove in to the university with her sketches, had quiet conferences in one office or another, ate lunch in one of the cafeterias around the science and medical complex, shopped a bit perhaps, or saw a friend, and then drove home.

Once she had felt drawn up to the fourth floor of the hospital past the room where Hanna had died; another child lay in the bed, and another mother sat in the green vinyl chair by the window. A shout of laughter came down the hall from the nursing station; a metal cart was clattering along a hallway out of sight. She didn't go back again.

She looked at children on the street, blond children, and at mothers who didn't seem to understand the full value of what was theirs. Once, in the checkout line of a supermarket, she had rushed away in confusion, leaving behind the basket of groceries, because of her overwhelming desire to pick up the child in front of her and hold her close, perhaps even to run away with her and to keep running until she could find a quiet place to talk.

She tried to tell herself that it was natural her sorrow should be taking these different forms, and that she must simply wait and accept its evolving transformations.

One late afternoon as she drove into their lane, a thick wet February snow was beginning to fall, windless, very still, like a false oblivion, and two crows were screaming over the catalpa skeletons at the bottom of the pasture. Her body was worn down by the last stages of the flu. John too had been ill, and she found him in bed, muffled in a shawl, reading, smoking his pipe. His clay-splotched trousers hung from a chair.

"You look ravishing and curative," he said as he stretched and threw aside his book. His stiff hair was raked up and the creases beneath his eyes looked personal and contemplative.

"I'm frazzled and sick," she said. "You're just playing the lascivious old man again; none of it is genuine." But she went to him and sat down close, laying a hand on his chest.

"Spending an afternoon in bed has had certain effects," he said.

"You've improved your mind and the state of your health, I hope."

"My mind has been rotting away with carnal lust. For you, of course, my dear," he added.

"You sound venereal," she said as she rested her weight against him. The play of their bantering went on by itself, remote. Outside the window the snow continued, thicker now and bluish. "Where are the boys?" she asked.

"I told them to go out and do the goats for you."

"That was nice." It was all distant, even the sadness, even the dried mask that was pretending to be her face.

They were snowed in the next day, and on the following noon Louie came with the tractor to clear the lane. He brought in the mail, standing huge and good-natured in the mudroom in his layers of sweat shirts and coveralls, talking about the snow.

"That was some snow," he said.

Catherine watched him trudge out to the corncrib. Once in the army in Alaska Louie's legs had gotten frozen from the knees down. Watching him work made her think of life as being a matter of putting one stolid foot in front of another, endlessly.

"Well, he's coming," said John, holding out a letter, "Laurits Jorgensen—that fellow I told you about. He's taken the apprenticeship and has agreed to twenty hours of work per week in exchange. How does that sound?"

"For how long?" asked Catherine. She read hurriedly down the paragraphs.

"Six months or so—we'll see how it goes." He sat in his ragged down vest, nursing his pipe and coffee and slowly working himself up to go out to the shop. It was a familiar sight. He had been up until four that morning with a firing.

"This is going to be good for you, isn't it?" said Catherine. "You might actually get the new kiln finished."

"He does say he's good with tools. He's a find, I'd say."

"You'll take him sight unseen?"

"I trust Merton—he wouldn't send a slouch."

"He'll get a room in town, I suppose?" asked Catherine, returning to her dish of fruit and yogurt. She had been up at seven with the boys and for most of the morning, while John had slept with the covers over his head, had been at her drawing board in their sunny bedroom.

"He could do that," said John.

Later in the afternoon he came in for a sandwich and brought it up to the bedroom. He squeezed the back of her neck, kissed her ear, and then sat down in the old wing chair. She heard him biting through lettuce and sucking from his can of beer.

"I've been thinking," he said as he set aside his empty plate and leaned back with the beer can balancing on his chest, "that fellow Laurits could take Hanna's room, if you'd agree. It seems a waste of time for him to go back and forth to town every day when he could just as well stay right here."

Catherine turned her pencil around and around in the sharpener. She squinted at the network of mammary ducts on her paper.

"We'd have to do something about the curtains," she said at last.

"That's simple enough, isn't it? It just seems to me that it's time now to start using the room; I mean, love, we've got to do it some day."

She heard the school bus on the road and looked out to the lane where Tom and Drew were jumping down from its steps.

"All right," she said slowly, turning back to her husband. "I think we could manage that."

II

"You must be Catherine," says the voice in the barn door. She turns from the fresh straw she is forking down and sees his shape against the light. It is April.

She goes over and sees him better. He has blond hair that is parted in the middle, and it hangs straight on either side of his face. His eyebrows are black.

"Then you're Laurits."

"The master there sent me out to meet you." He tosses his head slightly toward the shop.

She smiles as he smiles. It is one of the first warm days.

"This is quite a place; it's really beautiful. What else do you have besides goats?"

"Nothing, except a hundred or so cats."

"You own it all?" He is leaning against the old timbers of the doorway and looking out towards the undulating Iowa fields.

"Just the house and the barn and the shop. Louie has the land. You'll meet Louie before long." The pregnant goats are outside the door drinking from a trough. She has filled a large pan with grain. Now she heaves up a basket of old straw and droppings.

"I'll take that," says Laurits. "Where to?"

"That dung heap over there."

"This is fantastic," he says as he jauntily brings back the basket. He tosses the hair from his eyes.

They walk together toward the shop where they find John sponging smooth the rim of a large tureen. The reddish clay glistens like a moistened lower lip. Catherine has seen John take a finished piece like this, to her eyes perfect, and slice it relentlessly apart to reveal a slight inconsistency in the thickness of the form. There are other days when he is unable to work at all; then he might lie hour after hour in the darkened bedroom, harshly humorous against himself and the world. She has understood for a long time that her strength is different from his.

"Well," he says to Catherine, screwing his face above the pipe smoke, "the slave has arrived. Have you shown him to his miserable quarters?"

"Not yet," says Catherine, "he's been helping."

"That's good, lad. I'm glad to hear you haven't wasted these precious minutes cavorting aimlessly in the barnyard. It's work we want around here. Work! do you hear?" He makes his eyes look fierce and insane.

"Yes, sir," drawls Laurits. He has propped an arm along a drying rack and seems as much absorbed in the tureen as in either of them. Catherine wonders where he has gotten his confidence.

John seems invigorated, boyish himself. He stops the wheel and draws a taut string under the base of the tureen. "That's it," he says; "let's go talk about the future."

They are very gay. Catherine sees that it is a good combination of personalities. When the boys come home, they hang on the railings beside the porch swing, fascinated. Laughter gushes out over the lawn and the beds of spring flowers and freshly tilled garden. They are talking about the new kiln for salt glazing, about the distances to the surrounding towns, about the farm girls in the neighborhood. John allows himself a leer. "They grow up fast around here," he says.

A meadowlark is singing from the walnut tree by the lane, a piercing, slurred call that seems to contain the entire moment. Clouds are rapidly riding out of the west, fanning out into an expanse of sky and disappearing over the house. Catherine feels herself breathless at the spaciousness these approaching masses make visible. She is sitting on the steps with her coat collar up, hugging her knees. Tonight she will make a large salad with fresh mushrooms and chopped cress. Her mind is planning. She looks at her sons, and it seems weeks since she has noticed them. They are growing quickly. Their heads of identical brown curly hair are like lively, irrepressible masses of energy.

Later, in the night, she wakes and feels the house full of sleepers. Catherine turns her face into her pillow and smells her own hair. Her body is radiating heat, her cheeks feel smooth. Sometime during the night the first of the goat kids is born.

Laurits makes competent pottery, mostly smaller pieces like bowls and mugs and casseroles. He does not seem apologetic about what he has to learn. He listens carefully, and he is keeping a chart of glazing mixtures. When he sits at the kitchen table for tea, he turns the mug thoughtfully, sometimes holding it by the handle and sometimes cupping both hands around its belly.

Today he has come back from town with the onion sets Catherine has ordered. When he has made the tea, he calls up the stairs to her. He seems to like the kitchen. He talks to Catherine about an idea he has for building some shelves over the stove; getting up, he shows her how they would span, from here to here, with hooks underneath for pans and open space above for pottery. He has started to grow a blond mustache, and now when Catherine looks at his face she notices even more the darkness of his brows. She has stopped being surprised at how comfortable Laurits seems talking about these everyday household matters. He makes himself useful, but he doesn't seem to need their praise.

When they finish their tea, they go down the side yard together to the garden. They take turns making trenches with the hoe and placing the onion sets. Catherine has already planted radishes, beets, and carrots. Laurits says that when the time comes he will make some circular supports for the tomatoes from some old fencing he saw in the corncrib loft. He follows along beside her, pushing dirt onto the onions with the flat of his hoe. Catherine can feel the heat of the sun through her jacket, and she thinks that there are only seven weeks until the summer solstice. She has stopped being surprised at how comfortable she is working with Laurits; it is almost as peaceful as working alone, and yet even the simplest of motions seems to be enhanced. She is crumbling compost into the bottom of a trench, and her hands seem to be understanding exactly the nature of its richness. When she was a girl Catherine used to sketch her own hands, with wonderment, and now, remembering that, she seems to be reminded of the richness of her own nature. She straightens up to see Laurits at the edge of the garden, aiming walnuts up into the tree at the last few nuts still clinging to the branches in their green casings.

Laurits is reading in the rocking chair by the dining-room window. After lunch he always takes this rest; Catherine has told him he reminds her of her grandfather, and he has told her that he reminds himself of his own grandfather. She has come up the lane with the mail, and she taps on his window as she passes on her way to the shop. In a few minutes she returns to the house.

"You have two letters today, Laurits," she says. "I think your lovely lady must be missing you." The postmarks are from California. Laurits has said that her name is Leah and that she is studying marine biology. She is twenty years old; Laurits is twenty-three.

Laurits puts down his magazine and takes the letters. A Swedish ivy plant is hanging in the window above the library table; Laurits begins to read his letters beneath this cascade of scalloped leaves. Outside the window green maple-blossom discs drift in the sun.

Catherine sees Louie in the south field beyond the garden making a sweeping turn at the end of a row with the corn planter lifted from the ground; he drives with one hand as he twists in the tractor seat to gauge the beginning of the new row. Her own hands feel empty.

She pours herself a cup of coffee in the kitchen and goes upstairs to her drawing board. The bed is unmade, and the air is warm and still, almost like a summer afternoon. She is working on a schematic frontal section of the female reproductive organs, using books and charts loaned by Maxine, the biology professor. The new women's center has inquired about the publication date of this booklet; it will be used as well by high-school family-life classes and will be among the free literature available to incoming college freshmen. Maxine is in her late fifties. One of her daughters ran away from home at the age of seventeen; it was very bad for awhile, Maxine has said, but then gradually things worked themselves out. Catherine looks at her drawing and understands that what she is seeing is a section through a moment in evolution.

It is June. The boxes are packed, the van is loaded for John's Chicago fair. Today Tom is fifteen. They are having his party at lunchtime, before Catherine and John must leave, and while Tom assembles his new fishing gear, Catherine cuts down through the cake. John is at the other end of the table, waiting for the coffee to be ready. His effort the last few weeks has been tremendous. Even he has called himself a maniac. The kiln has been fired twice a week. His final project has been a series of huge vases, almost human in their forms, with gentle bellies and flared rims and handles akimbo—his vestal vessels, he has said, giving one of them a pat.

He works at his pipe and squints at Tom; Catherine can see him searching for a humorous attack: no son of his is going to come off easily from a birthday.

"That's pretty sophisticated gear for a young whippersnapper like you," he says.

"Whippersnappers are good at things like this," says Tom as he carefully fits together the sections of the rod. He is barely suppressing his excitement with the gleaming tackle and newly fitted-out box, all chosen by his father, everyone knows. Laurits has promised to take the boys catfishing and camping overnight on the river. Drew watches everything from a calculated slouch.

"So, Laurits," says John, "do you think you can keep these lads in line? No ruckuses on the Mississippi?"

"We kids will not besmirch the family name," says Laurits. "Simply think of us as young gentlemen off on a naturalistic holiday."

"Mind you look to the goats before you leave," says John to the boys.

Catherine pours the coffee in silence. She is disorganized; her bag is scarcely packed. She is remembering the long labor of her first son's birth, her partial disbelief that it was actually happening . . .

"Now there's a well got-up woman," says John to her later in the bedroom. "The brow, the bosom, the lovely thighs—a figurehead for our ship, worthy, if you pardon the expression, of breasting the crest. Together, my dear, we will navigate the evil city and bring back lots and lots of money."

"John, will you please be quiet? You're exhausting me."

"I'm exhausting you?"

"How was I exhausting you?" he asks on the highway.

"Just talk straight now, all right? We're alone, there's no one listening."

"We are alone, aren't we?" he says that night in the hotel, smiling down at her. City sirens pulsate on an eerie stratum of air, disembodied. All night there are voices and shouts, neon-light waves. Catherine does not feel that she is sleeping, but then she wakes, terrified for the safety of her children; in a moment she remembers that one child is already dead. John sleeps curved and dark.

The bathroom is white, white everywhere, but she can only think of the thousands of people who have touched its slickness without leaving a mark. She sees that her period has begun: her skin, their toothbrushes, and the brownish blood are the only colors in the room.

She sleeps again, floating on sound and the sensations of her body. Hanna is calling her on the telephone, a child's voice, difficult to make out. Yes? she says to her. Yes? Speak up! Everything but her own voice is indistinguishable; the telephone cord is slowly disintegrating. She wakes into the morning.

"This hasn't been too bad for a rickety-dinky hotel," says John, pleased with himself.

He is opening the curtains. "Will you come with me to the village square, my love, to peddle our wares?"

She puts on a large straw hat and over her swollen breasts a white blouse, open at the neck.

The week before Laurits had worked bare-chested in the garden, and she had seen that he was smooth and compact, self-contained. He had knotted a red scarf around his brow, and his back had glistened.

"Come on, lass, let's get a move on," says John.

Movement: she must move in spite of herself; she can no longer be in last week's garden, bending over vegetables.

"Are you all right, love?" asks John in the coffee shop.

Outside in the street the light is too bright; there is too much light, everywhere; even beneath the mottled plane trees at the fair she finds only an overexposed confusion of dapple. She hides beneath her hat.

"You're quiet, love," says John after he has made another sale. Year after year many of the same people return to his booth. Catherine looks up to see the face of Dr. Avakian, inviting them to dinner that night. She feels herself nodding. Dr. Avakian has greyed remarkably in the past year. He and his wife live childless in a high apartment near the lake. Catherine knows all about the evening already; she can see the iced wine, the crepes filled with crab, the fresh strawberries, the strong coffee and pastry in the living room above the reflecting water. Each year Dr. Avakian buys two, perhaps three or four hundred dollar's worth of pottery. It is obvious that he considers himself a patron and that he must search for ways in which to spend the money of his middle age.

Catherine presses her knuckles into her eyes. The innards of her body are heavy and sinking toward the gravity of earth; within and without the world seems constructed of motion and loss. She tries to imagine her sons in a rented boat at the mouth of a Mississippi slough; what she sees is Laurits, selecting bait from a bucket.

As they speed home across Illinois the next afternoon, the landscape for many miles outside the urban fringes seems tentative and barren, as if it had already lost its vigor in the face of the impending lava-creep of the city. It is not really until the Mississippi itself that Catherine begins to relax. Looking down from the bridge, she sees the wide river flowing effortlessly between its banks and feels reassured, as if she herself had caught an easier current. Inland John turns onto back gravel roads and they approach the farm into the sun, beside newly cultivated corn rows that look like giant thin-man legs running with the car. Catherine opens her window and takes a full breath of earthy air; she feels the presence of her heart.

The weather turns very warm. At the end of the month Tom and Drew prepare to take a bus out to camp in Colorado where they will ride horses, backpack, and fish for trout.

"I hope those whippersnappers appreciate this," says John as he closes the van on their gear.

Catherine takes the pipe from his mouth to kiss him. "Take care of yourself in that big-town bus station."

"I plan on being alert," says John. "Not a hussy will pass my notice."

"You sure know how to talk big," she says, feeling his arm around her. The boys are in the shop saying good-bye to Laurits. The yard is still and empty except for scattered dozing cats, and yet Catherine thinks that perhaps she and her husband are being observed. He seems charming and inscrutable, and as she lets him shuffle her through a few dance steps and lower her into an embrace of mock passion, she finds herself looking up with alarm into his grinning face.

"John," she says suddenly. "Maybe I should come along for the afternoon. Do you want company?"

"I thought you wanted some precious solitude."

"I did. I do." She looks at her watch. "There really isn't time to get ready."

"Look," he says, taking her by the shoulders, "I'll take care of our sons, and I'll take care of myself, and you take some time for yourself the way you planned. all right?"

Catherine stands silent in front of him, and for a moment his mannerisms seem to fall away, and what slams against her is his suffering.

The boys come loping across the yard from the shop.

She wants to touch him. Her throat tightens into pain. Hanna! John!

Laurits follows slowly behind the boys, wearing a rubber apron, his forearms and hands reddish.

"The troops are assembled," says John, and the moment has passed.

Catherine kisses her sons, everyone is joking, and then the doors slam and the van pulls away.

"I hope they get some good trout," says Laurits; "there's nothing in the world like mountain trout."

Catherine nods. She goes inside the back door and presses her fist to her mouth. "O, my God," she hears herself whispering, "O, my God," and she feels that her hands are being flung, taut, above her head. And then she picks up a rainjacket from the floor and puts it back on a hook. In the kitchen she watches her hands finishing the dishes. When they are done and the plants hanging above the sink have been watered, she takes down a sketchpad from the top of the refrigerator and goes out to the side porch. She draws the walnut tree and in the foreground the trunk of the wounded maple. Then she goes down to the garden and sits close to a pepper plant, letting her pencil understand the way the white blossoms are giving way to tiny green buds of fruit. She is sitting on a mulch of straw. Not far away a yellow and black spider is zigzagging a reinforcement in his web between two tomato plants. It is almost too hot to stay where she is, but she continues, turning from the peppers to the fuzzy eggplant leaves, and then to the squash vines and nasturtiums. For a long time she feels as if only the motions of her hands are keeping back the tears; then gradually she begins to forget about everything but the nature of what she is observing. At last she takes off her shoes and lies back on the hot straw.

All around her are the rustlings of insects or of plants growing. A hawk circles several times overhead and then banks out of sight. She shields her eyes with a forearm smelling of tomato leaves and herbs.

She doesn't know if she has slept, but at an indeterminate moment the air has changed; a faint cool dampness has swept the garden. She sits up. From the south a mass of round white clouds is approaching rapidly; from the north a front of blackness is bearing down with amazing speed. It is fascinating, she thinks, and the heat, thank God, will lift; then an instant later she knows the danger.

"Laur-its, Laur-its," she yells scrambling into her shoes and running to the shop. She throws the sketchpad inside the screen door, shouting, "Laurits, a storm is coming," and without stopping further heads for the small goat-pasture behind the barn. "Here babes, here babes," she calls to the already frightened animals. She has to lift the kids over the stone sill of the barn. One door after another she runs to secure; the cloud masses converge as she is struggling with the huge double doors of the barn's central passageway. Laurits appears beside her. By the time they are running for the house, a whipping rain has begun. A trash can sails across the yard, then a tree branch.

They tend to doors and windows. The house is moaning, the windows rattling, the metal weather stripping whining above even the high-pitched fury of the storm. Outside the air is greenish through the almost horizontal slant of the rain. A bolt of lightning to the west appears to stab a nearby field; thunder shakes the house. Laurits thuds down the stairs with a blanket around his neck. He takes her by the arm—"Upstairs is all right, let's get down"—and they descend into the basement fruit cellar where the hundred-year-old lime foundation stones are damp and motionless. Laurits sinks down underneath a workbench and opens his blanketed arm like a wing for her to enter.

They are in one of Hanna's old forgotten playhouses, one of the many hideouts that she had fashioned for herself around the farm. This one consists of a few peach crates beneath the bench, set up as shelves, and on the floor a mildewed playpen pad. The child had tied some yarn around one of the crates as a sort of decoration, and inside Catherine finds a canning jar filled with rotting kernels of corn and one large spider, alive. She puts it down slowly. The mind of her child seems near enough to touch.

Catherine cannot stop the tears now; she feels that she has never been so close to her sorrow. Lowering her forehead to Laurits's

knee, she lets herself become a rounded shape of grieving. "Hey,"
he says, "hey," as he begins to stroke her hair and back. Her body is
wracked by an accumulation of feeling, as if the sobs are coming out
of her bones. "Catherine," says Laurits, "here, here." He has
taken her close to him in the cramped musty space; from upstairs
comes the faint screaming of the wind. "Catherine, what is it, what
is it? There, don't talk. Catherine." His hands over her ears are
muffling all sound. Her brow is being stroked; he is kissing her eyes.
They are underneath a storm, in a space made by a child. "You're
having a bad time," says Laurits, holding her head against him. She
is snuffling now and breathing more quietly; her brain feels as if a
searing connection has been made between its two sides, leaving
behind a warm fluidity. "That's better now," says Laurits. She feels
herself being rocked slightly; with her eyes closed she has a slight
sensation of weightlessness. Laurits is cupping her breast with a gentle hand of comfort.

"There now," says Laurits after a time. "Let's go upstairs and
see what's been happening. Do you think it's safe?" He wraps the
blanket around them both and pulls her in close against him as they
start up the stairs. "Catherine," he says, stopping halfway up to
kiss her hair. He lowers his forehead to hers, and she lets her hands
rest upon his chest.

They go from room to room, window to window. The yard and
lane are strewn with tree limbs, and one huge branch has crashed
down through the electrical wires to the shop. "Laurits, that's a hot
line then, we should call," but when they go to the telephone, those
wires are silent. They test random lights and all are dead. In the
wake of the lightning and thunder and furious wind is now a heavy
turbulent rain, being blown in thick curtains across the fields. The
light inside the house is a brownish chiaroscuro.

Laurits sits down in a chair against a kitchen wall. Catherine goes
across the room and sits beneath the useless telephone. They are being careful now. "I'm going to guess that for you there has always
been only John," Laurits says quietly.

"How do you know that? Do you find it strange?"

"I think I would have expected it."

"It's not that I haven't loved others, but well, yes, there's been

only John. We moved from place to place; we went through a lot
together. And then, too, I've been a mother for a long time." She
draws an uneven breath. "You must understand that has something
to do with it."

"You don't have to apologize."

"It's different for you?"

"Literally, yes, but I've told you, Catherine, I'm my own grandfather; I'm not sure where I belong."

"And Leah?"

"Leah? Leah is like water, you could say she follows her own
natural laws. She's living with someone else this summer."

"I had no idea," says Catherine. "Is that all right with you?"

"I take large chances," says Laurits. "She's a brilliant girl; she's
absolutely set in her scientific interests." In the half-light Catherine
watches him shrug. "We'll see," he says.

"And meanwhile, back at the farm?" she asks gently.

"God, Catherine, don't mock me—are you mocking me?" He
comes and stands in front of her. "Answer me." He is smiling.

"I'm not mocking you, Laurits. It's just us, here; I'm seeing it
all."

He hunkers down in front of her and circles his arms around her
hips. "Why were you crying? Can you tell me that?"

She tips back her head against the wall and feels how close the
tears still are. Images are welling to the surface: the face of John that
noon, the layers and layers of his reality; the countless vibrant expressions of her daughter, her lovely child; her own life, obscure
essence, visible movement, change, desire.

Laurits has laid his head in her lap. "Come on," he says, "we
can't talk here." He lifts her to her feet. "Come on, follow grandpa." He leads her up the stairs and into Hanna's room, his room,
and to the same bed where the child had first wakened in the night
with the pain—a headache no mother's hand could touch.

"Laurits—"

"We'll be good. Just talk to me." He covers them both with a
light blanket. "Just tell me." He opens her blouse and lays his cheek
against her breast; she can feel the steady waves of his warm breath
across her nipple. She strokes his hair and begins to talk. She tells

him about the hospital, the days and nights that became indistinguishable, the one resurgence of hope when the child's eyelids fluttered and her mouth seemed to be straining to speak; she tells him about the dreams, how she is certain that the child's spirit is present, that the other side of death exists even though it's untouchable; and then she is talking about John, about the days when he cannot work at all and his mockery turns inward and consumes his energy and her own as well, about the way the death has cut through their marriage to reveal a section-view of bewilderment barely concealed by stylized action—not that they aren't tender, not that there isn't pleasure in each other and in life: it's just—how shall she put it—it's perhaps that a reality has been given them that they haven't been able to incorporate yet; it doesn't fit into the old patterns. Does he understand, is she making sense at all? And then she realizes that it is herself she is talking about, grieving for: the inability of her hands to help her child, the weakness of her mind to understand what is now happening, the confusions of her heart. Her voice continues. She doesn't know what is coming next, she simply doesn't know, and she is asking herself, will she be able to live it?

When John returns at dark, they are in the kitchen making supper in candlelight. He is drenched from having run up through the rain from the end of the branch-choked lane. "The survivors!" he exclaims, coming to the stove and putting an arm around each of them. "Did you know, my children, that you have only narrowly escaped the fate of Louie's great-aunt?"

"We haven't had any radio, John," says Catherine. She has laid her own cheek against his wet one.

"The tornado touched down four miles north of here."

"That close!" whistles Laurits.

"Was anyone hurt, John?" asks Catherine.

"No one reported, but I saw damage to buildings, and lots of trees."

"What's this about Louie's great-aunt?" asks Laurits.

"You mean you haven't heard that story yet?" says John. "Catherine, love, I'll leave you to the telling while I go get dry and then may I suggest a bottle of wine for this murky night?" He shudders dramatically in his clothes.

She lays a hand on his arm. "And how were the boys? Did they seem to feel all right about leaving?"

"They couldn't wait to get away, and that's the honest truth. They said, bye, Dad—that's all, just bye old Dad." John waves his own hand in farewell and soft-shoes himself out of the kitchen.

Catherine begins to set the table.

Laurits is looking at her. "So? the story?"

"Well, once upon a time Louie had a great-aunt. I don't know her name but she lived in the days of high button shoes. Now this great-aunt was caught up in a tornado, picked up bodily; and she was finally found in a field two miles away, unhurt but covered with scratches and bruises, her hair was a mass of brambles, and—here's the crazy thing—the wind had left her absolutely stark naked except for one high button shoe."

"One high button shoe?" repeats Laurits.

"One high button shoe."

"She was lucky. But she must have been mortified."

"So to speak."

They are laughing, and it is a great relief. The thought of Louie's great-aunt being propelled naked through the air with one external item of dignity intact is exactly the image they need for the end of this day, in this world of astounding variety. "What a story," says Laurits, whooping, breathless, and then he says more quietly, "but she must have blacked out, surely the force of the wind must have knocked her out."

"I suppose so," says Catherine, and she pauses above a sliced tomato. "Tell me, Laurits, if you had your choice, would you go through a tornado like that conscious or unconscious?"

"Good God, Catherine," says Laurits, "I'm going to make you answer that one yourself."

III

One hot afternoon in September while Laurits and John were testing the new kiln, Catherine took herself for a walk along the back roads of the section. There had been no rain for weeks, and the hushed crops and weeds were coated with a film of dust from the baked roadbed. Catherine strode along in spite of the heat; her body was strong from the months of outdoor work, and she felt vital and continuous to herself beside the stretching fields. The landscape to some eyes would have seemed monotonous, she supposed, but she was coming to exult in its apparent plainness; here her eyes could spread out, rested, and her mind could empty itself, and she could be seeing nothing but straight road, fields, fences, and predominant sky until one detail—a changing of light, the thwacking up of a pheasant from a thicket, or a stream of water, invisible from a distance, cutting through the surface fertility—would simultaneously define for her both the plainness and variety of her surroundings, like the first stroke on a sheet of blank paper.

Today she was thinking how much this vast swelling land seemed to have retained its character of primordial ocean floor, and her own eyes were seeing it: the knowledge of a progression through millennia to this present moment of late-summer dry lushness and quiet was passing through her, making her a special child of the universal elements. She stepped off the road and sat down in the minimal shade of an Osage orange tree, looking up with curiosity at the globs of wrinkled greenish fruit. It was true: she felt almost like a child, and what was more, she was gradually understanding that her own lost child was being returned to her, not as she in her suffering had dreamt of the reunion, but simply as she herself was moving to the embrace.

She rested until she became thirsty, and then she got up and continued on the last two-mile stretch, lowering her eyes slightly under the sun, tasting dust on the dryness of her lips; and but for this chance direction of her gaze, she might have missed the dead frog: levelled by a car in the dust of the road, it was like the perfect shadow of a leap, yet really there, paper-thin and dried, complete with flattened eye sockets and delicately spread feet. She bent down to study the creature, her own shadow a foreshortened shape beside her on the dust; and toward this desiccated carcass that like a hieroglyph said purely, *frog,* and toward the even more cryptic configuration of herself she felt a quickened outpouring of that which long ago had come to be called love.

Small Voices

He is running. Every day he takes himself out into these old residential streets and runs until his fingertips throb, his legs radiate heat, and the whole of him begins to ride on a steady rhythm of his own making. He once tried to explain to his wife that he wouldn't know what to do with himself unless he pushed through these physical barriers. His body is a wonderment to him. He thinks a great deal about his spine, about all the muscles that are necessary to keep it erect. Sometimes he cannot believe the height of himself as he stands in a doorway; he feels so huge it is as if he should be able to take a single step and understand everything.

Today he is running in the hour before a spring sunset. All day, believing and not believing that his life is really happening to him, he has been bending to his work in a fastness of books and papers, surrounded by what his wife called, before she left, the fall-out of their confusion. She said she no longer had the will to move the stale objects of their existence from one place to another, it was too dangerous, and so she was going to do the only thing that remained: take her attention some place else. The curved dried shell of the orange she was eating that night still sits on the windowsill beside the bed, and the pillow he slammed against the wall lies shapeless, feathers of dead birds.

Once he had raised his hand in fury against the unaccepting, slack beauty of her cheeks, her wounded past, but then stayed himself and rolled away trembling, his body curled around its own apparent uselessness. He still cannot believe that what he offered her was not a relief from the long catalogue of her hurts. These days he finds himself scrutinizing other men, the ancient wrongdoers, his tribe. Evenings since she left, he has been keeping to himself, trying to purify himself from the rhetoric of combat.

He runs past a blur of cradle-like wooden porches, airy forsythia, a red wagon, an old woman bending upon a rake, houses containing an inconceivable number of lives. Lately his own life is taking all the energy he has; he is almost relieved that she is gone. The new running shoes he has bought himself are of soft white leather with bright blue stripes. His legs are long and hard—he likes his legs. When he has finished running, he often feels as if he has come out on the other side of where he had been before; even the disorder seems rearranged, workable.

It used to amaze him on his returns that his wife would be as he had left her, reading and chewing on a hank of her hair, sending out silent messages of self-containment. He remembers how after a time she would set aside her book and without a word go the kitchen for something small to break her hours of fasting—a jar of baby fruit, perhaps, or a slim wedge of cake. Many of her habits were defiant and unhealthy. The activities of his body seemed to irritate her.

These last ten days of solitude, testing himself for damage, for damage done, he likes to think that he is purging himself of whatever does not naturally belong to him. Never has he enjoyed his runs so much. When he comes back, cleaned out, on the edge of himself, he fixes himself good dinners and sleeps well. The woes of history are beginning to seem unnecessary.

He has reached the point at the bottom of the hill where five streets join, and he takes the old brick way, toward the graveyard. At the arching ironwork gate he spits and shakes his arms and continues on up the curving drive past angels and obelisks and fenced-in family plots neater than any dream of ordered domesticity. The sun suddenly clears the last of the afternoon clouds, slanting richly across the bright green grass and sharply delineated markers, and for a moment his breath swells with the illuminated clarity of this customary place of obscured bones and feeding trees. His parents are buried in another cemetery, a thousand miles away.

He sees the feet first, in sandals, then legs in slacks, a piece of what looks like raincoat, the rest blocked by granite. Thudding up the hill anyway, curiosity stronger than embarrassment, he passes a jar of wilted lilacs, a ten-foot angel frozen in prayer, the granite square, and comes upon a woman stretched out on a grave in the shadow of the stone. Her face in its nest of curls has color, her eyes seem to be moving beneath their lids. He stands watching her chest for breaths. One of her hands rests on her stomach, the other lies half-open at her side, the veins in her thin wrist like surfaced roots. Inscribed in the headstone are the names Agnes, dead the year before at the age of sixty, and Raymond, already cut into stone but still living somewhere beyond the incised hyphen. The young woman sleeping does not look anguished. Her features are peaceful and fine. He wishes he had a blanket to put over her, and shivering himself as a drift of cooler air passes over his heated body, he turns to complete the far curve of the drive and then the long westward descent. The sun jogs and flares through the trees on his downhill lope. Strange to have seen an unknown woman asleep like that, unaware of who sees her; strange to be running half-blind straight into sun motes and bright new green, not knowing who knows you are flashing through gravestones bare-limbed, twelve feet high, muscles and bones gathered perfectly together for motion, a young man spectacularly going somewhere with himself.

He almost crashes into her at the iron arch. Her hair is spun out into filaments of light.

Sorry, he tells her, sorry, he had the sun in his eyes. Is she all right?

She looks at him as if maybe she were still dreaming.

He saw her asleep, he explains. Is she all right?

She was exhausted by her drive, that's all. Thanks. She is turning to go, but she smiles at him. He remembers a photograph he saw once, taken into the light, of a woman with the same slightly aquiline nose, the same burst of fine hair, geraniums silhouetted on the windowsill, the inclined face gracious and complete. He wants more than a smile.

Her mother? he asks, nodding to the graveyard.

Yes, her mother.

He pauses. He's sorry about her mother. Where's the dad?

Not here, not underground, she answers, and not in his office either, which would be the two most likely places. She had driven down to surprise him, but evidently he is gone for a few days. She shrugs, she seems to be collecting her breath.

She doesn't live here then?

No, she doesn't. She is regarding him. But he does, from the looks of it, and he's shivering. She has taken car keys from her pocket.

He wants more. He wants a face like hers to incline itself to him graciously and completely. Stepping in place to keep warm, shaking his arms, impatient, he is suddenly feeling sorry for himself for his days alone. After all, was it not his wife who did the leaving? This woman seems to him nomadic, accessible. His new running shoes work gently up and down on the walk, he flaps his arms. She could give him a ride if she's going up that hill, he says, dramatizing his chill. In fact, as long as her father is gone, he could give her supper, humble of course, but he's always happy to help a traveler, been one himself often enough.

She shakes the keys, considering. All right, she says. Supper.

She drives slowly, and he leans back and lets the closely set houses trail away on either side. The car is their own container. The wind has been taken off his skin. He rests his hands on his knees and lets himself be transported.

Where has she come from? he asks.

She has been visiting some friends. Actually, this time of year she usually travels for several months, staying with people, freeloading. Summer is the busy time.

Summer?

A gift shop, she answers. She has her own little place. And many of the people she visits give her craft items to sell on consignment. She nods to the crowded back of the car. Some beautiful things come out of the dark winter, she adds. She grins at him merrily. Does he have anything he'd like her to sell? pottery? dried herbs? jams? candles? jewelry? She makes good deals.

He bets she does. In fact, she doesn't seem hard-nosed enough to make a cent.

Oh, everyone is mellow enough, she answers. It all works out. Sometimes she trades.

He directs her down the alley to the back of his house. Fantastic trees, she tells him as she faces up into the oaks spreading new leaves above the unkempt yard. Nice old neighborhood.

He feels he should prepare her for the shattered mirror in the bathroom, the unwashed plates and dying plants. He has been tending only to the direct minimal needs of his mind or body, touching what had been communal only when necessary. Once or twice he has even thought of removing himself from the debris, simply taking his plain, healthy body and leaving.

Well, too late, she's already halfway in the door, and how on the round earth anyway was it possible to turn one's back? This is where he lives, he says squarely, the ruined castle, the unattended kingdom.

It is a mess, she agrees, standing on the threshold of the back door. What's been wrong?

He begins telling her about the restless anger of his wife. He carries a frying pan from the stove to the sink and sets it to soak. He wipes crumbs from the oak table and flourishes a chair for her. His wife is brilliant, he says, and he's no dull head himself, yet neither of them seems to be able to put the lids back on jars, to attend to the simplest things. Now why is that? he implores her, opening his palms. His words are light, he is making himself charming, but he is waiting for this young woman shedding her raincoat to absolve him from a verdict of banal catastrophe. He sits down and stretches out his magnificent legs; he crosses his arms over his chest and clamps his fingers into his hot armpits.

She is wearing a black jersey and a necklace of silver and turquoise, her hands, too, are studded with turquoise. She has begun to nibble from a bag of nuts and raisins on the table, her face tilted to one side as if she were listening to the air. Her eyes are laughing at him.

He looks as if he's capable of putting lids on jars and sweeping up a bit, she answers. In fact—she slides her fingertips under her hair, pulling taut the skin over her forehead and temples as she surveys the room—well, why not tell him, she says, because it looks as if it's happening again, though this is the first time with a total stranger, and so she'd better explain herself before she gets to work. But first—and here she gets up and goes into the other rooms; he can hear her opening and closing a few doors—she comes back and announces that it can be done in an evening, but first he has to bathe, no first he has to show her where a few thing are. She has opened a cupboard and is picking among its scattered holdings.

No, first she has to tell him what's going on, he demands. He is standing up now, tall, beside the table where he had once laid his wife, and he still believes she was laughing as he hooked her legs over his arms; he can't remember when exactly the laughing stopped, nor when the arm shot out to throw the lamp against his chest.

She'll tell him as they eat, she insists; now if he'll just find her the rice and tea.

He stands naked beneath hot water. His own parents were crushed in an automobile. For three years his mind has been replaying images of the crash; he has been reaching out to touch their faces, but his hands come away bloody, unhealing. In the night his mother's ghost, still searching for completion, comes to the window and watches his face lying on the pillow. At first his wife was interested in his sorrow. They both had griefs, she said. Then she began to suggest that being an orphan was not at all like being the victim of a century of repression. Nursing her elbows, she would tell him how girls were belittled even by their own fathers and mothers, so where was the hope? The power of men to corrupt was inescapable, she said, and those they corrupted first were the women who remained at their sides. Therefore she was leaving, now, before there should be children, heaven forbid, and while she still had the vision and the strength.

When he is clean, he dresses and goes to the kitchen and says, Tell me.

She says, All right. She is frying vegetables. I don't know when this all began really, but I became conscious of it the spring my husband and I separated. I was staying with friends, looking for the right place to live and feeling far away from what I needed. I went to sleep one afternoon and dreamt about a passageway through evergreen trees. The next day I drove back into the countryside—everything was alive, plowed up—and I came to the opening of a long lane bordered on both sides by fir trees, and on the top of the hill was a simple old farmhouse—for rent, it turned out, with exactly the right views of fields and timber, exactly the right emptiness and the right light. My mind would spread out.

She sits down with plates of rice and vegetables. She pours tea. With my husband that somehow wasn't possible, she says. The doors seemed closed, only the smallest part of me was being used.

Well, anyway, after that other things began to happen. I'd get an urge to go visit a friend and when I'd get there I'd know a crisis was going on—I mean, you can tell—she gestures to the kitchen. It was as if I was meant to have arrived. So I would do what was necessary. I'd help out, you know. I have begun to travel more and more, I don't know what's going to happen. She puts down her fork and holds her long ringed fingers for him to see. I feel instrumental, she says. The power collects when I'm alone—the solitude is very important—and then when I come out with people again it all flows out here, through my hands.

He runs his forefinger lightly across the tops of her hands and then turns them over and looks at her palms.

Are you spooked? she asks, laughing.

Do you ever make love? he asks.

Sometimes. There's a schoolteacher up in my town who wants to marry me.

Will you make love with me? He feels the shapes of her rings against his palms.

I'm going to clean your house, didn't you know? You're going to clean, too, she says.

All night?

We'll see. She has withdrawn her wealthy hands to her tea.

We both have dead parents, he says.

Her eyes are on him, above the poised steaming cup, and he tells her about going home to the empty house, letting himself in through the basement door, climbing to the silent kitchen, finding his mother's notes to herself, family pictures, light angling up the green couch, ashes in the grate, upstairs full drawers, coins on a dresser, a dish of pearls with a broken clasp. He went through the drawers, he says, he smelled everything, like a dog, he put his fingers in her box of pink powder and wrapped a nightgown around his neck, noticing that it needed mending, that it was really a very old faded nightgown with torn lace. That night he slept alone in his down bag inside the attic dormer of the house, the casement open to the stars. He remembers putting his tongue on the zipper of his bag and tasting metal as he fell asleep. He remembers that once long before that he had wanted to push his father out a window.

She is acknowledging him over her cup.

I've never told that before, he says.

You're all right, she says.

My wife thinks I'm lethal.

She shrugs. These are difficult times for men and women, she says.

After they finish eating, she goes to her coat pocket for a scarf to tie around her head. First she takes all the plants into the bathtub to spray them down and pick off the dead leaves. He stands in the doorway and watches the bones of her spine as she bends over the decimated collection.

Some hope here, she says.

Together they stack up the scattered books and newspapers and shake out the old oriental rug that covers the day bed. He goes to start in on the dishes and trash. Occasionally he hears her singing from the other rooms, simple tunes in a slightly nasal voice.

In the webbed circles of light from the table lamp, he sweeps the floor, then draws a bucket of water and begins to scrub. As his arm rotates over the mottled floor, the gesture seems to him like a repetitive blessing over the surface of the earth. He is a tall holy man in bare feet, beneficient after all, perhaps. Now and then he looks down the curve of his chest to his crotch. He is crying. Each time he lifts the rag it comes away filthy. Once he hears a tapping on the window and glances up to see her smiling in at him from the night. She comes to the back door with an armload of stolen lilacs. The beauty of the world belongs to the people, she says. She puts one small jug of purple on the table, says nothing about his tears, and carries the rest of the blossoms into the living room.

When he has finished the floor, he blows his nose and goes to find her. She has moved the rocking chair closer to the couch, he notices, and set the lilacs on the low table. The washed plants are back on the window-sills, looking stripped and fragile. A pile of dirty sheets and towels has been gathered in the hallway. The space itself seems altered, feasible. His head feels close to the ceiling, his body enormous, faintly weightless in the dim passageway, and at its end the lighted bathroom door seems attainable by a single step.

He finds her picking away the last of the mirror shards from the cabinet frame. In place of those distorting reflections of anger she has affixed another mirror, small and round, surrounded by a sunburst of gilt paper. Something from my car of treasures, her voice says. She is leaning close to the mirror, her eyes are on herself, but he does not know what she sees; his own sight seems to slide off her form, he feels a pulsing inside his body. He does not know how to reach the other side. She must have looked into the centers of other mirrors in other places, pulling down her scarf in this same way and raking her fingers outward to the ends of her tangled halo of hair, turning to one person or another in the background, with the flecks in her eyes appearing yellow, unmined, luminous with her own tears; yet will she be smiling this way, her attentive jeweled hands raised open to the air exactly so, her same voice chanting that sometimes she too feels like a motherless child, a long, long way from home?

In the Land of Plenty

Margaret had been working nine months at the New Life Food Cooperative when her husband came back to town. She hadn't been expecting him; she had been trying not to expect anything from anyone. Simplicity was her desire now: to care for her two children, to get enough sleep, to pay the rent. Her present life was such a surprise to her, so unimagined, that in her abashment she felt ignorant, remote from her own future. Many dozens of faces came up the stairs to the store each day, and it was her job to stay still and let their needs flow through her mind and into her fingertips; when she went to pick up her children each afternoon, joining these streams of people, she tried to keep herself compact, her own needs minimal. She felt peaceful on nights when she was able to go to bed at the same time as her children, especially when she might wake up at midnight and understand that she had already slept for three or four hours and that a full passage of rest remained. As she went back to sleep, the undemanding night would seem to be caring for her, perceptibly, but beyond her knowledge.

The afternoon that Sloan came up the stairs of the co-op, reports had been blowing in with customers of a bitter shift in the weather, a temperature drop of at least twenty degrees and a stupefying icy wind. Margaret had been listening to Mimi and John joking as they stacked away produce in the walk-in cooler about the coming of another ice age, not two thousand years hence, but now, brothers and sisters. Mimi, dressed in her usual plaid flannel shirt, her long hair braided, had been throwing twenty-five pound bags of organic carrots through the doorway to the lanky, down-vested figure of John, astride crates of lettuce and broccoli in the cooler's interior, and in their exuberance they seemed to Margaret exempt from catastrophe. She herself was at least ten years older than either of them, she had children, her father was dead, her education incomplete, her marriage a bewildering disappointment, yet she listened to them companionably. Never, before this job at the New Life, had she felt so comfortable and accepted. She liked the large upper room with its bins of grains and seeds, its shelves of herbs and spices and coolers of dairy products and fresh produce, she liked the section of useful, invigorating books, and she liked the people, Mimi and John, and Carl.

"Yes, it's coming," said John. "This here cooler is nothing compared to what's coming."

"Do you know what's really going to happen?" laughed Mimi. "We're all going to learn to lower our body temperatures and live forever."

"Naw, we'll just change into something else," called John.

Margaret rang up a customer and went back to stocking the herb jars. She heard Sloan's drawl before she saw him.

"Is Margaret around?" he was asking.

"Margaret the True is yonder with the herbs," said John's voice.

She tightened the lid on a jar of anise stars and put it back on the shelf before she turned around.

"Hello, Sloan."

"Stump said I'd find you here." He glanced around the store, and when he turned back to her, Margaret noticed the network of bright red blood vessels on his cheeks and nose, like frail explosions. He smelled of cigarettes. "How's business?"

"Very good," she made herself answer casually. "We're going to open up a bakery." Sloan looked sickly. At the thought of what he might have been eating and doing to himself, she took down a jar of peppermint tea and began refilling it carefully from a large plastic bag.

"Working hard?" asked Sloan.

"That's right. How have you been, Sloan? Stump told me about California. That's too bad."

"Yeah, well, that's just one of quite a few that didn't work out." He pulled out a cigarette.

"No smoking here," she said briskly.

He looked at her hard, and his skin seemed to flare out at her. His blue eyes were watery and bloodshot. Then he eased away the cigarette and looked around again. "Not bad up here. It's pretty damn cold outside."

"That's what we've been hearing," she said. She took down a depleted jar of cinnamon quills with unsteady hands.

"How are the girls?" asked Sloan.

"They're all right. They're in school, of course." She tipped the jar to keep the cinnamon vertical. The quills looked like rolls of brown parchment, curled around secrets.

"I'd like to see them," said Sloan. "I'd like to spend some time with them." His voice had risen slightly.

"When would that be? It's the middle of the week, and they have to have their sleep or they'll get sick. You could have written ahead." She bit down on her lip and lowered her eyes. It was the eldest girl, Helen, who missed her father the most. They had been pals, of sorts; he had taken her places. He was fond of saying that his daughter had saved his life once, when she was only five and he was as low as he had ever been. She had held his hand all night, he said, until the drug wore off, and what a miracle it had been, the touch of that child. It was a story Margaret always heard with a tight heart, for she had never been able to tell what a nightmare it had been to her not to know where her child was, for four hours, six hours, twelve hours.

"I could stop by tonight," said Sloan. "I'll pick up a pizza or something."

Margaret shuddered. "That's all right," she said quickly. "I'll feed them. You could come by around six-thirty. But they've got to be in bed by eight."

"Hey, look, what is this? I haven't seen my girls for over a year." He spread out his hands and drew out the words as if he had rehearsed them. "All of them," he added.

The jar of cinnamon slipped from her hands and shattered on the floor, quills rolling under the weighing table and against the base of the shelves. *Coriander,* said a jar near her eyes as she bent to pick up one of the larger pieces of glass.

She wasn't sure if Sloan helped clean up the mess or not. John appeared with a broom and dust pan. Several more customers came in, and an elderly woman asked her where to find the bran.

"I'll be around then," she heard Sloan saying, and he was gone.

She looked up and saw the wooden ceiling fan at the head of the stairs wheeling slightly.

"So that's the old man?" asked John as he gave a last sweep.

"Flesh and blood," she answered and held out her hands for the broom and dust pan and bag of glass. "I'll put these away if you'll mind the register for a few minutes."

"Take what you need," he answered.

In the partitioned office at the back of the stock room, high above the sloping alley, Carl was still working on the books as Margaret slid into the old school desk by the corner window. A gull rode by on a blast of wind. Roof tops down the hill and towards the center of town seemed in this weather to be turning human life in upon itself. The fear of what she might have done or was still doing to deserve her husband bore down on her. She lowered her eyes to the scarred surface of the desk.

Carl turned a page and she felt his eyes on her. "You're quiet," he said.

"Speechless," she agreed.

"And you look a little peaked."

"My husband was just here."

"You didn't know he was coming?"

"No, I've been trying not to think about him at all. He never writes, I've told you that." She looked across the shabby room at Carl, upright now above the ledger book, his eyes intent on her.

"Why aren't you divorced?"

"I'm not sure how to go about it. I haven't any money. I thought maybe he'd never come back."

"You're afraid of him."

"What do you know!" she suddenly exclaimed. He sat composed and solitary in the grey light; he lived in two rooms; he had no responsibilities other than to himself, and these he took seriously indeed: he was going to medical school; he was going to transform the profession with ancient wisdom; he was going to teach people how to eat, how to exercise, how to be quiet. He glided in and out of the co-op, performing his job, helping with policy decisions. "What do you know?" she repeated, but less angrily. She felt her spirit draining into the afternoon's bluster.

"Not too much," he said finally.

She drew an uneven breath and looked out again over the town. "I'm tired," she said. "One of my children had bad dreams last night. I was up more than down." Then she was silent, because what she was not saying was that she herself had also dreamt, had wakened from the dream, and had not been able to sleep again: she had been nursing a child, a baby adept and ravenous in suckling, and her milk had been instantaneous, prodigal, a miracle of abundance. When she had wakened, and the pleasurable flush of the dream had given way to the realities of her life, she had sat up with confusion in the cold room, wondering who in the wanton recesses of her mind could have been the father of this child. Its infant desire had been so strong and so easily fulfilled by her! The action had been so simple!

"Why don't you go home then?" asked Carl.

"No, I've got to wait until my children are out of school anyway."

"So. What about your husband? Does he stay with you?" Carl had taken an almond from a bowl on the desk and was cracking it with his teeth. He lifted out the kernel and chewed thoughtfully.

"No," she said firmly. "No, he does not."

He will not, she repeated to herself later that afternoon as she pushed her way through the weather to the grade school where Helen and Sarah were waiting inside the glass doors, behind circles of breath frost.

"I have a stomachache," complained Helen.

Thoroughly chilled, Margaret stood for a moment inside the door, working her feet up and down on the rubber mat and shaking life into her hands.

"Can you walk home?" she asked her eldest daughter.

"I'll try, but why does it have to be so cold?"

"I wish I knew," answered Margaret as she bent to tie little Sarah's scarf.

"How bad is your stomachache, Helen?"

"I just don't feel good."

"Well, let's get on home. You might just be hungry."

The wind drove against them a biting, granular snow. Bending into it, Margaret felt her energy reaching out to encircle her children. She wanted to gather them to her, to spread her arms and sweep them home, to have them instantly warmed and fed and safely at rest. The cold on her forehead was like a mark; she bore it; she was their mother, she told herself, their mother. Then she remembered that she hadn't told them about Sloan. The mark of cold seemed to concentrate itself, to radiate from her head into a zone of defiance. When men like Sloan chose to default in the care of their children, then there had to be certain forfeitures; there had to be.

Her fingers were so numb she was barely able to unlock the door. The children collapsed onto the couch. "Get your boots off," she said. "Here, wrap up in this blanket until the place warms up." Her own voice returned to her in the sparsely furnished room. She went to turn up the heat. She hung up her coat and put on an old sweater, and then she came back to the couch and began rubbing the girls' cold feet.

"Your father is in town," she said.

"Daddy!" shouted Sarah.

"Yes, he'll be stopping by tonight to see you."

It was almost too much, she saw, for Helen especially. She sat silently, her eyes full of tears, looking at her mother, and then she overlapped her coat carefully on her knees; she knotted her fingers; she pressed her lips together in an expression so unchildlike that it frightened Margaret.

"How long is he going to be here?"

"I don't know. I only saw him for a few minutes this afternoon."

"Mother, are you going to get a divorce?" The child's body remained rigid.

"I don't know that, Helen." She tried to speak soothingly. She tucked the blanket around them. "Now I'm going to get supper started. We'll see if that doesn't help how you feel."

"I want Daddy to stay home," said Sarah as she burrowed deeper into the blanket.

Kneeling before them, Margaret looked uncertainly at the package she had made of them, tucked up, mothered. She turned on a light beside the couch and without a word went down the hallway to the kitchen. How had Sloan done it? Without lifting a finger he had their love.

In the kitchen she breathed deeply, measuring her strength. The old alarm clock on the counter ticked metallically; five, perhaps six hours stretched between herself and the release of sleep. She turned on the red-shaded lamp on the table and the light above the stove. She rinsed the alfalfa sprouts and watered the fern above the sink. Gently she shook its fronds. This was her room. Small triumphs bloomed in this kitchen. There were curtains; the cupboards had been painted brick red; more plants grew on the windowsill; there was a new toaster; there was Black Cat, who jumped down from the chair beside the radiator and placed himself in her path. Margaret fed the cat. She stood in the middle of the room, staring at his body crouched over the bowl and thinking about the number of hours in each twenty-four that this animal slept.

Sloan was unbelievable. What did he expect of her? She felt confounded by memories.

She cooked an omelet for the girls and carrots and whole wheat noodles, food that they liked. She gave them slices of homemade bread and quartered apples for them and poured their milk and watched them eat. What she longed for were actions simple or humble enough to cleanse away the taint of having lived with Sloan, of having chosen to live with Sloan, of being connected to him still and not knowing what to do about it. Her mother had warned her, but Margaret had taken a last look at that pinched, anxious face and gone away. These days her mother sighed to Margaret on the long distance telephone, or wept; life was out of control, she said, but at least she and Margaret were finally reconciled, there was that, though how it was all to end, who could possibly tell? And those poor fatherless girls, she had added.

Margaret ate a little of the supper. "Can't you eat more, Helen?" she asked, but the child shook her head.

"How long until Daddy comes?" she asked.

"Half an hour or so," Margaret answered. "Why don't you get ready for bed now so you won't have to spend time on that while he's here?"

"I don't want to. Maybe he'll take us somewhere."

"Not tonight!" Margaret swooped upon the words. "It's bitter, bitter cold. You can't possibly go out tonight. You, Sarah, don't you want to get cozy in your pajamas? I'll read to you while you're waiting."

"No," said Sarah as she pushed a last slice of carrot through the butter on her plate. "I want to do cartwheels."

Margaret got up and cleared away the plates. She flooded them with water. She scoured the table with her dish rag and slammed shut the cupboards. She swept the floors. "Out!" she said to Black Cat, "out of the way!" and she swatted him with her broom.

"Mad Meg," her father used to call her with amusement when she was angry, and simply knowing that he was thinking about her, even through the artificial sympathies of alcohol, she would feel some of her frustrations dissipating.

Margaret put away the broom. Wind whistled in the back door. Downstairs was the furnace; upstairs two medical students slept in the rare hours when they were at home; outside stretched a nondescript vista of frame duplexes, a featureless corridor along which the wind had been whirling hollowly when they walked home. Twenty years her father had been dead. She put water on the stove for tea, took her books from the top of the refrigerator and sat down at the table. The idea of death ballooned in her mind.

She could hear Sarah thudding now and then in the living room with her cartwheels. Helen she imagined to be lying on the couch, with a library book perhaps, nursing images of the reunion with her father. Margaret opened her book deliberately and ran her hand over the smooth pages. This time she was not going to allow herself to be angry with Sloan. When she looked at him, she was going to remember that this year she had found out what it was like to go to bed with a feeling of innocence, with no regrets for the day; to be on speaking terms with oneself; to close one's eyes like a child.

She bent her eyes to the book. She was reading about the life cycles of ferns, and next fall she was going to take a few classes. Why shouldn't she, Carl had said, since she was always reading anyway. Pressing her breasts against the edge of the table, she examined the circular diagram that was the journey of a fern. Last night in her dream her breasts had been translucent, and she had been able to see the milk streaming down to the child. She had been sitting in a tub of warm water while she nursed the baby, a stout wooden tub in the middle of a warm room, and she had been holding the child securely against her bare body, just above the level of the water.

It had been three o'clock when she woke up from the exotic fullness of the dream into the starkness of her room. In spite of the cold, she had been damp with sweat. She had put on a dry nightgown and gone to cover the girls, stepping over ghostly toys in the night light, bending low over their beds, but the usual reassurance to her of this motherly action was missing. Something seemed to have been cut loose, a connnection. Back in bed, she huddled alone, adrift and sleepless on a night that had lost its effortless and soothing progression. Who was this strange child? Where was the source of her abundant milk?

Folding her arms over the biology book, she laid down her head, close to the smells of wool and paper.

Startling sounds woke her, shouts, the kettle's whistle, footsteps. Leaden, she dragged her head up. It was all happening. Slouched in the doorway, Sloan had already insinuated himself into the heart of the house. The children tugged at his old leather jacket, begging to be lifted up. She saw it obliquely, dimly, she had the sensation of being unable to straighten up or move; her hair straggled against her cheeks; her jaw felt slack, dream-weighted.

"Your kettle's going off, Margaret," he drawled.

She swung her eyes to the stove.

"Helen," she said, "can you get the stove?"

Sloan had entered the room. His eyes roved, taking stock. Sarah jumped up and down at his elbow.

"Not now, babe," he said, blowing into his hands. "Give me a minute to warm up."

Slowly Margaret straightened her back and leaned her head against the wall, her hands folded over her book. She saw him flick the fern and run a forefinger over the new toaster.

"Looks like you're getting a little ahead," he commented. He rocked on his heels. "Looks real homey here." He pulled one of Helen's braids. "You know how to make coffee yet?"

She shook her head. "I can make scrambled eggs."

Helen looked challengingly at her mother. It was all happening. "Go ahead," said Margaret, "we've got eggs." She made herself stand up and go to the stove. She measured tea into the pot. "We don't have coffee, Sloan. Do you want to sit down?"

He hung his jacket on the back of a chair and picked up Sarah. "You're getting big, babe, you know that?"

"I know that," said Sarah. "And guess what!"

"What!" said Sloan.

The child's six-year-old voice giggled, halted, and began again, "You know what?"

"Do you want toast, Daddy?" asked Helen. Her cheeks were flushed.

"Watch the heat under that butter," said Margaret. She returned to the table with the teapot. It was ten minutes to seven.

"You know what?" said Sarah.

"What!" repeated Sloan, leaning back and bouncing her on his thigh. He looked amused, and Margaret felt her own face to be flat, exhausted. Sloan had on a clean, checked shirt.

"What kind of witch rides on a gold broom?"

"Dummy!" cried Helen bossily from the stove. "You've said it wrong."

"No, I haven't."

"Yes, you have. You gave it away. You say, 'who rides on a gold broom.'" She brought a plate of eggs to the table. She fetched salt and pepper, toast and butter and sat down importantly.

"Helen," said Margaret, "that wasn't necessary."

Sarah had hung her head. Now she climbed off Sloan's lap and came to hide her face against Margaret.

"Well, she always gets them wrong," said Helen, shrugging her shoulders and smiling self-consciously.

Margaret felt a panic rising in her. She took a sip of tea and stroked Sarah's head.

"Tell us again," she said. "Who rides what?"

Sarah shook her head and pressed harder against Margaret.

"What's the answer?" asked Sloan, his mouth full of eggs. "Somebody tell me."

"Well," said Helen, "the person is supposed to ask who rides a gold broom, and the answer is—"

"Stop it!" screamed Sarah. "That's my joke."

"Well, tell it then," said the older child.

"No." She was crying now. Margaret gathered her up. She felt helpless, bound to her children, yet ineffectual.

Sloan pulled out a cigarette. "What are you doing these days?" he asked Helen.

"Reading," returned Helen quickly. "I read lots of books from the library."

"You do, huh?" Sloan was squinting at her over his smoke. "You going to grow up to be a reader?"

"I'm going to write movies, like you."

Sloan snorted. He poured himself more tea and glanced briefly at Margaret. Then he took a dollar from his pocket and tickled Sarah behind the ear. "Come here, babe," he said, "I've got a trick with this dollar. Let me see if I can get it right. Come on, get your face out of your mommy so you can see George Washington here. Ok, you see this dollar? Now, I'm going to fold it over once, lengthwise."

Helen leaned close to her father, following his hands. Sarah was watching sidelong, snuffling against Margaret.

"Ok now, you fold it again. Let's see, am I doing it right? Now, what's going to happen to old George is that he's going to turn upside down. See that?"

"Let me try!" shrieked Helen.

Sloan looked again at Margaret.

"You've learned a few new tricks?" she asked.

"That's an old one," he said. "And yourself?"

"No tricks," she answered.

"Ah yes," he said, stretching back, "still the same."

Restless, he surveyed the kitchen again, and Margaret felt her life diminishing.

"What are you reading?" he asked, nodding at her book.

"Introduction to Biology."

"That's a new one, isn't it?"

She shrugged. "I liked biology before I even knew you, Sloan."

"Ah yes," he said carefully.

"Show me again," said Helen, as she held out the dollar.

"Let's go spend it, girl," Sloan said suddenly. He put the dollar in his shirt pocket and slapped a hand over it. "Go get your coat and you can help me spend it."

"Sloan, please, no, don't take her out tonight. It's much too cold. She had a stomachache this afternoon. You can't do it. Look, it's almost her bedtime." Then she looked at her daughter's face and fell silent.

"Simmer down, Meg. One ice cream with her old pa isn't going to kill her. How about you, babe?" he asked Sarah. "You going to make up to me? You want an ice cream?"

"She does not," Margaret said quickly, holding her youngest child closely on her lap. "She had an ear infection last week, and you're not going to take her out."

Sloan whistled dramatically and shrugged into his jacket.

"Mama, please," begged Helen.

Margaret pressed her lips together and closed her eyes. She was in a corridor; she was being dragged along a corridor of whirling voices, and wind, death-cold. An icy defiance gathered behind her eyes. The stiffened membrane of her lids opened and she looked fixedly at Sloan.

"How long are you going to be in town, Sloan?" she said coldly.

Sloan whistled again and stared at her.

"I said how long," she repeated harshly.

Sarah had begun whimpering again.

"I'm going to get my coat," said Helen desperately. She looked from one parent to the other. "Don't yell at each other. Daddy, don't get mad." She tugged at his hand.

"All right, all right," he said, pulling out another cigarette. "Now go get your coat."

"You can't keep on doing what you're doing to that child," said Margaret in a low voice when Helen had gone down the hall.

"I'm not doing anything to her. I'm still her father. She understands me."

"She does not. She's a child, with the needs of a child."

"Well, what do you want me to do?" He gestured broadly. He dismissed the kitchen with a single fling of his arm. "I couldn't possibly work in a place like this. I can't play your little games. That kid understands me better than you ever will."

"I told you I play no games," said Margaret, her voice rising. "I'm simply trying to raise my children."

She felt Sarah's body tighten in her arms.

"You want me to apologize, is that it? You want me to say I'm sorry I didn't get the money to you? Look, I didn't have a cent, I didn't have enough to eat myself."

"I don't care about the money anymore," said Margaret wearily. Her moment of angry energy had passed and she looked dully across the room at the person she had once willingly followed two thousand miles from her childhood home into a day-to-day excessiveness that had become more alarming and enervating than any of the strictures from which she had escaped.

"What do you want me to do?" Sloan repeated in a loud voice.

"I don't know." A blankness was passing before her eyes. She thought of sleeping; she thought of being in her bed, with none of this happening, the night unfolding gently, everyone safe, everyone good.

"You could get her home by eight o'clock," she said finally.

Helen was standing in the doorway. She had remembered her boots and scarf. Her bluejeans and coat were too short, her mittens unmatched. She wore the red hood that Margaret had knitted at Christmas.

"Eight o'clock," enunciated Sloan, slapping his heels together.

Margaret saw Helen put her hand in Sloan's as they disappeared down the hallway. The house shook with the closing door, and Margaret shivered, as if she herself were facing the wind.

Sarah's body had slumped over in her lap. Margaret lightly touched her lips to the soft center of skin and neck curls between her braids. Lifting up the child's face, she kissed her cheek; she kissed the tearful eyes; she pressed her lips against her hair.

"I wanted to go," cried Sarah. "I wanted an ice cream. Daddy likes Helen best. He didn't want me to go."

"There, there, you can blame me about the ice cream because I didn't want you out in that wind. Now come on, let's get you to bed. I'll read to you."

"He does, he likes Helen best. I can't stand it anymore. I can't stand being a little sister."

Margaret lifted her up. "You'll feel better when you've slept."

Sarah was almost too big to carry. The motions of putting her to bed seemed to contain all that Margaret had ever done for her children, the countless garments that had passed through her hands, and the dishes of food, the weights that she had carried, the nights alone when she had bent over their beds, constrained by Sloan's vagaries to an austere constancy that she had gradually begun to embrace gladly, as a possible means of separating herself from him, of redeeming herself from her own follies.

"There now," she said, pulling the covers over Sarah. "Shall I read to you? Shall I finish the one about the king and the princess?"

"No," said Sarah, her voice still catching from her tears, "tell me about when you were a little girl."

"I think I've told you all there is to tell."

"Then tell me again." She clutched at her blanket.

Margaret sat down on the edge of the bed in silence. She rested a hand on Sarah's knee. Across the room the covers on Helen's unmade bed were twisted and empty. Margaret had taped many of the children's drawings to the walls. She remembered the Saturday she had done it, how she had been making soup, how she had washed the girls' hair, how together they had made a board and brick bookcase and straightened up the room.

"I used to say my prayers every night," she said unexpectedly to

Sarah. "I used to put my head under the pillow and pray to God to be with me."

"When you were a little girl?"

"Yes. I don't know how old I was, nine or ten, I suppose."

"Like Helen."

"Or maybe I was six." Margaret leaned close to her daughter. Two of her teeth were missing, another half grown in. Her face was quieter now; it looked as if a hand had passed over it and smoothed out the contortions of sadness.

"Did God come under your pillow?" she asked sleepily.

"I don't know."

"Tell me more."

"Close your eyes."

"Tell me about when you were six."

"Every winter my legs got chapped and they burned when I got into the bath water."

"Just like mine. What happened?"

"Someone would put cream on them."

"Your mother or your father?"

"I don't remember. Now go to sleep. You're almost asleep."

"Stay here with me."

"I'll stay until you're asleep."

"Go get Black Cat. Please. Make him sleep with me."

"I don't know where he is. I'll look for him in a little while and bring him in."

Margaret turned out the light and sat for a long time on the end of the bed, listening to the wind outside and the sheltered breathing of her child. Where was Black Cat, she wondered. She had hit him with the broom, and where had he gone? Her face tightened with the pain of her own weakness, her mistakes. Noiselessly she began to get up from the bed, but Sarah said, "Stay," from a deep layer of her sinking consciousness and so Margaret felt herself assuming again the shape of a mother, waiting. The image soothed her a little.

Once at the age of twelve or thirteen she had had a friend whose mother she had loved. This woman has passed into her like a light, sometimes over the years forgotten, brightly to reappear and remind her of a value possible perhaps even for herself. As a girl, locked in the bathroom, she had caught her own profile in two mirrors and pondered the seldom-seen contours, looking for a similar distinction.

"It's that damn way you hold your head," Sloan had gibed one night with his hands around her neck and his thumbs overlapped lightly on her throat. "Don't tell me you're not like the rest of them," he had said.

Margaret knotted her hands. The room was growing colder. This time when she stood up Sarah was silent. Out in the hall she blinked. "Black Cat?" she said at the door of her own room. She snapped on the light, but bed and chair were empty. In the living room she pulled the make-shift drape, a bed spread, across the street window and folded the blanket on the couch.

Sometimes he slept on the rug in front of the bathroom radiator, sometimes he went to the furnace room and scratched in the dirt where the old well had been filled in.

At the head of the basement stairs she called his name again, and her voice met the low breathiness of the furnace that was like a faint, steady underground wind. "Black Cat?" She went halfway down the stairs. The furnace labored hypnotically inside its box. "Here, kitty, kitty," she said, sitting down and resting her forehead against the railing.

"You can't tell me anything," Sloan had said. "I know you too well."

She seemed to hear his voice laughing in the upstairs hallway, as if it were all happening again. "Good girl," he was taunting, "good girl, good girl, good girl," and she hadn't known whether to laugh or cry because the worst part hadn't come yet, the worst nights were still to come, and she had let him push her up against the wall because she was still listening for something else, a softening from bravado, an inflection she could trust, a moment of clarity that would explain the power he had over her.

Without sound or color the cat came to her out of the darkness and jumped into her lap. "Here you are," she said vaguely. She put a hand around him and felt the way his breath swelled and sank.

Upstairs a door seemed to blow open, but there were no footsteps.

"Helen?" she called. "Sloan?" She ran up the steps and through the kitchen. It was nine o'clock. Wind cut along the hallway. The front door was open, and in the light from the street a million brilliant particles of snow swarmed expansively. Gripping her sweater over her throat, Margaret looked up and down the vast night before shutting the door.

In the freezing cold of the hallway she covered her face with her hands and was startled by her own substantiality. Sloan was uncanny. Like a shadow he had returned and in a moment the walls of her life had been displaced. What was she doing wrong that she should be so far from home?

At ten o'clock she rose numbly from the couch and walked the strange spaces to the telephone in the kitchen and dialed Stump's number. She knotted and unknotted the cord as she waited for his inscrutable, wheezing, corpulent voice. The phone rang again and again. Sloan had no other friends. Finally she put down the receiver and whirled around to face her own vacuous kitchen and gaping hallway.

Once before she had called Carl about a meeting at the co-op, and now she found his number without trouble. His voice answered immediately, a full, intimate vibration near her ear.

Not to worry, he answered. He'd take a look downtown. They were probably in the Pizza Palace or someplace like that. Red hat? All right. Yes, he knew what she looked like.

She thanked him in a deadened voice. She thought of his rooms where she had gone once with Mimi, their spareness and order, the bowl of oranges.

Hey, he said, hey, she was to take it easy, all right?

All right, she heard herself answer. Her shaking hand clattered down the receiver.

A moment later the front door opened, and Helen came in alone, muffled, frosted, her face barely visible.

"You walked!" Margaret rushed to her. "Where is Sloan? You're frozen! Where is he? Come to the kitchen."

Margaret led her along the passageway. She turned on the oven, and before its open door unwound the child's scarf and began to peel the stiffened garments from her.

"Helen, Helen, where did you walk from?"

"From the drugstore." She was crying. Tears had frozen to her cheeks. Her lashes were hoary.

"But where is Sloan? Why isn't he with you?"

"He was."

"But where is he now?"

"I don't know."

"What do you mean you don't know!"

"I don't know!" the child wailed.

Margaret said nothing more. She fetched a blanket. She warmed a cup of milk. She took her daughter into her lap and sat until her shaking had subsided.

"Can you sleep now?" she asked.

Helen shrugged.

"Do you want to tell me more?" Margaret pressed, frightened by the child's downcast silence.

"I don't want to talk about it," she answered theatrically, and Margaret winced. She shuddered with an unspeakable impulse to hit her child; instead she picked her up, long legs dangling, and carried her to the bedroom, where in silence she helped her into pajamas and tucked her in.

"Helen," she began, sitting on the edge of the bed, but she found no words.

Across the room Sarah sighed in sleep. Margaret bowed her head with her own fatigue. Helen had turned her face to the wall. "May I lie down with you?" she asked.

Within her embracing arm, Helen's body felt elongated, stretched far beyond its solid babyhood into a new condition of bones and hollows. The bed was close to an outside wall against which the wind continued to moan and thud. Margaret pulled the covers higher and lay breathing on the pillow close to Helen's hair. There had been other nights when she had slept with her children, in one narrow bed or another, when their bodies had seemed like islands of comfort and goodness in the turbulence of her marriage, nights too awful even for anger, when she had locked herself in the nursery and laid down her own destiny alongside those of her children, wherever it was that they slept cradled, and she had dreamt of beginning again, herself rich, abundant, at peace. Some nights she had almost stopped being afraid.

Helen's breathing was gradually slowing. Margaret felt herself loosening into sleep; she felt pieces of her mind returning home, sinking down.

There were footsteps, and she dreamt of being asleep and trying to wake. She heard voices. The door might or might not be closed. She was slobbering. Dragging herself up, she explained in a drugged voice that she could barely see her visitor because her eyes were still sleeping. In response, a wave of joy engulfed her, then another and another. A presence was appreciating her; miracle of miracles, she was loved. Everywhere there was dimness and snow, and now she was searching for a place to sink down with this new presence in the light of an eternal understanding, almost within reach. You can do it, said the voice, come where I am, and for an instant she did, weightless, bathed in an expanding stillness of delight. And then she had to go hurriedly down some wooden steps to slog through a heavy snow. The truck was leaving.

When the doorbell rang, she started up instantly from the bed, her body pulsing with alarm.

"Yes!" she cried, "yes, who is it?" She ran in stockinged feet down the hall. The lamp still burned in the living room. She had no idea of the time.

The door was opening.

"Any luck here?" asked Carl's voice.

"Carl!"

"I've looked in the most likely places." He kicked his boots against the sill and stepped into the gloomy hall. Inside the hood of his parka his face was barely visible.

"She came home."

"That's good! No worries then?"

"I've troubled you." She peered into his face. "I'm so confused tonight. I fell asleep just now."

"That's good. Go back to sleep, that's what you need."

"I don't know where Sloan is."

"Where he's staying?"

"He didn't bring her home. I don't know where he is."

"Wait a minute. What does the kid say?"

"Nothing. She couldn't talk. She was crying, and then she turned stony."

Carl loosened his hood and drew her into the light. "Now step by step," he said, but there was little more that she could tell. She huddled ashamedly inside her baggy sweater.

Carl was silent a moment and then he began to unlace his boots. "I'll sit a little while and warm up, if you don't mind."

"I'm sorry to be troubling you!"

He shrugged. "You've got some idea that you're not worth it, don't you?" He shed his parka and began blowing into his hands. His eyes were on her.

"It's just that all of this, tonight, before, it's not the way I want to be living."

"I know that." His eyes seemed to be taking her in.

She straightened up. "I'll make some tea," she said and motioned him towards the kitchen.

Would she tell him about her husband, he asked.

What about? His past? Their marriage?

Anything.

Carefully she was warming the teapot and readying the mugs. She felt a need to be deliberate, accurate, to think about what she was doing. Heat for this water came from the gas that also fed the furnace that warmed the water that coursed through the two apartments that were formed of walls, separating outside from inside.

Her husband was not easy to talk about, she answered. What he said, what he did, what he appeared, were not the same. He hated domestic life. He had had two complete families, two wives, two sets of children, both abandoned now. He was suspicious of anybody whose life wasn't at least half sordid. Oh, what could she say? She measured the herbs precisely and set the tea to steep, keeping her hands around its warm belly. Persuasive, that's what he was, amazingly persuasive. He was very good at getting you just where he wanted, and you never realized what pressures there had been until afterwards. And he liked to experiment with himself. He couldn't stand for things to be the same. What more could she say? He was almost completely unreliable, that went without saying. He was cruel. He was kind. He was very good with children, when he wanted to be. He hated women, probably, she wasn't sure.

Her eyes were staring into the slow emission of steam from the pottery spout, and then she shifted quickly to Carl.

Well, she asked him with a strained laugh, was she a fool?

He had no answer beyond his steadfast gaze, and her voice rushed on as she carried the honey pot and tea to the table. She wasn't used to talking like this, she said, he shouldn't let her go on because then there'd be no stopping her. A couple of years ago in Texas she had had a girlfriend and she had been able to talk to her about all sorts of things, it had been such a relief, but Sloan had put an end to that; he had done that friend, sure enough.

"Done her?" asked Carl.

"So that she hadn't the face to come back," Margaret rushed on. "He hated to see women together. Witches, he called us. He never let me answer the telephone first when he was at home."

She stopped, exhausted, and dropped her forehead to her arms. "Have you heard enough?" she asked.

"Have your tea," he said, pushing the mug close to her hand.

"You haven't heard the worst part," she broke out. There was no holding back now this cataract of words. "The first time was after Helen was born and I was sitting in the bed nursing her and he brought this guy in—he said he was an old friend, but I had never seen him before—and he sat on the edge of the bed talking to me and then Sloan went out and left us, and the whole time the baby was beside me on the bed." Her head dropped again to her arms. She rolled her forehead against her sweater. "There was another time, too," she cried. "And what could I have done? Who was I to tell? I had no strength."

And then her voice changed. She heard its stridency but was unable to stop. "Aren't you sick?" she asked fiercely. "Aren't you sorry you've come this far? Aren't you just sick? Don't you want to walk right out of here?"

"Hey," he said, "hey, I'm here because I want to be."

"I'm sorry," she said. She brought the mug of tea to her lips with both hands. Her body was sustaining deep, internal twitches, as if nerves were being jammed. Now and then she shuddered. "I don't think I was brought up very well," she said shakily. "Sometimes I look at people who know how to act, and I feel so desperate, I can't tell you. I've kept thinking all this year that maybe if I could just stay quiet long enough, I might learn how to live."

"That's a possibility," he answered.

"Talk to me," she implored. "Why do you just sit there letting me make a fool of myself? Tell me something. Where were you born? Did you have parents? What are you really interested in? Let me hear the sound of your voice."

He laughed. "What am I really interested in?" He poured more tea for both of them and slowly spun a spoon of honey for himself, and then he looked at her directly. "What I'm interested in is perfection. Perfectability."

"Perfection?"

"That's right. The richness of us all. We don't know it yet."

"Some people are richer than others."

"No, not absolutely." He smiled at her, and she felt suddenly cleansed by a gush of relaxation. The warmth of the tea had spread to her cheeks.

"I've had the strangest dreams the last few nights," she murmured. "But you keep on talking. I like hearing your voice."

"You're getting tired, I can see it."

"That's the doctor in you."

"Anybody could see it."

"I've got one more thing to tell you. Something just made me think of it," she said. "Once when I was about twelve I got sick at a friend's house in the middle of the night. My fever went terribly high," Margaret continued dreamily. "My neck was so stiff I couldn't move. It was pneumonia. All the rest of that night the mother of my friend sat beside my bed. She had turned on a little light, and she sat in a chair close beside me until it got light. My parents were gone somewhere, I don't know, maybe my mother had to drive my father to the hospital again. Every time I came to myself and opened my eyes, there was my friend's mother. I was very frightened of my delirium, but I could always come back to her face. It was a life line, it was, I can't tell you what it meant to me. I felt as if no one had ever been so good to me." Margaret rested her jaw in her hands. Her eyes were beginning to close.

"She kept watch," said Carl.

"Yes, she kept watch. I'd never had a gift like that before, at least it seemed that way."

"That's a beautiful story," said Carl. He finished drinking his tea in silence.

"I'll tell you what," he said, fitting the lid back on the honey pot, "you go on in and go to bed—you're halfway there already—and I'll stay a bit in the living room. I'll stay all night if you like."

"That's too much for you. You've got classes tomorrow."

"Never mind. I want to see what it feels like to be the mother of your friend. Now go ahead, I'll turn out these lights."

All her weariness was rushing to its conclusion. "All right," she consented, "I don't know what else to say."

"Nothing more now."

He led her down the hall and left her at the door of her room. She heard him running water in the kitchen. She heard the basement door closing. She heard the footsteps of the upstairs dwellers, coming home. She got in between the covers and lay floating downstream in the half-light from the hall. A shadow layered her course. "I forgot to cover the girls," she said aloud. "And I promised Sarah she could sleep with the cat."

"I'll do it," said Carl from the doorway, and the shadow moved.

Then it passed over her again and Carl came in and sat down beside her.

"They're covered," he said. "Do you want anything? A drink of water?"

"No. Thank you."

"I'm going to pull up that chair and sit for a little while."

She acquiesced, already asleep, and then she swam back and opened her eyes. He was sitting with his legs outstretched, his arms folded over his chest. The light was on his forehead.

"Carl?" she said heavily.

"Yes?"

"I want to say something."

"All right."

"I hope nothing has happened to Sloan."

She saw him nod reflectively and lower his gaze, and then she was given the blessedness of rest.

Trio

Now they were deep into the frozen months. If Paul and his two daughters were a few minutes early to the piano lessons, he would nod to the secretary of the music school, and they would wait in the comfortable office where it was warm. Here the radiators clanged and hissed against the disparate music of three or four or five violins and pianos, one of which might now and then, like a voice, swell momentarily above the others as the door to a lesson room opened and closed. Outside the ground-level window a bare hedge of spirea had become bowed down with ice.

He usually sat on the couch, one daughter on either side of him, the feet of the youngest in her rumpled knee socks not yet touching the floor. Sometimes the children rested their heads against his arms; they were tired from school, and it would be dark by the time they finished their lessons and were driven home. Paul's own eyes were often heavy as he waited. Thoughts came and went in the space of his mind—about his lectures and papers, one student or another, the laundry, the groceries, the book he dreamed of beginning to write in the summer, the hope of a letter from his wife, Marta—but for the time being it was a relief simply to be quiet with his children, the pressure of their bodies against his like two stabilizing weights.

The central fact of their present life, which Paul woke into each morning and took with him to bed at night, was Marta's separation from the family for the year while she finished a lectureship in the eastern part of the country. He and she had reasoned long over this decision, weighing the esteem and usefulness of careers and salaries against the sustenance of daily family companionship, until one day early the previous spring Marta had admitted that she actually felt insulted by all the friends and family who were just assuming that she would break her contract and follow Paul to his new position in the Midwest. Where was her own voice, she had wanted somewhat shrilly to know, and from the increasing extremity of her language, Paul began to accept the depth of her need for separate action. So it happened that he not only went on ahead without her, but took the children with him as well. Intelligence, they both hoped, would see them through.

For Paul it was a good deal messier and more lonely than he had allowed for. If he had been alone, he would have thrown himself into his work in his usual way and so have pushed on to some sort of familiar sense of order; but in this year of solitary responsibility for the children, his attention was so divided that he often lost his former dynamic momentum. Haphazard complexities could absorb huge amounts of energy. Action seemed muddied. From the low vantage of his periodic exhaustion, the future would loom up as alarmingly demanding and circumscribed.

The piano lessons, however, were somewhat of a relief. He found that he was looking forward to them. His job was simply to sit off to one side of the piano in the parent's chair, listening to the music and taking down a few instructions for the children's practicing at home. The lessons took place in a small upstairs room off the stage of the chill auditorium. Besides the grand piano and the chairs and a case of music, the other furniture in the room was a box-like gas heater, which in this season sucked a low note of wind into its internal fire and occasionally vibrated sympathetically with the piano. Dusk would come during the hour of the lessons. Outside the tall, arched window was a sycamore tree, reminding Paul pleasantly of his studies in Europe; between these mottled limbs and scattered brown seed balls he measured the dark blue approach of evening.

First Marie, the youngest daughter, and then Kate would come upstairs for instruction. Carol Harper seemed to Paul a very good teacher. Energetic, professional in spite of her youth, a trifle nervous perhaps, she used herself effectively on behalf of the children.

She asked questions and waited when replies were slow; she taught music theory so naturally that it began to bloom even in Paul's mind; she moved the children's fingers to the correct keys without too much comment; she praised; she encouraged; she was humorous and yet precise about mistakes; she was reverent. The idea of music seemed marvelously at large in the room. Paul instinctively appreciated the excellence of the teacher and the orderliness of the lessons. A great deal would seem to have happened inside a small space.

He found himself thinking more and more about music and about the economy of beauty. His own family had never had a piano, pehaps never had even considered it. A close, unadventurous lot, of whom he was the only outlandish and far-flung member, all their efforts had gone into making him, the only boy-child of their four, a scholar, so that he could win scholarships and thus gain a more material hold on the precarious, fearsome tenancy they called life. Both his parents had been the children of immigrants, from Sicily, but they had probably never imagined his eventual studies abroad, his unclannish marriage and the peripatetic careers of both himself and his wife. His parents never travelled themselves; in not one of the young couple's half dozen domiciles over the years had they ever ventured to visit.

Striving in large measure there had been in his past, but little music. These days Paul found himself fascinated as he supervised his daughters' practicing each night. Slowly, with fingers that felt thick and slow, he learned to play the simple pieces himself and felt their shapes take hold in his mind; when he finally came to the first Bach minuet and could read it through, he felt tremendously happy. He played the scales, too, and listened to their different sounds. At the lessons he sat humbly and quietly, stayed from his own busyness, while his children nimbly played. Their large, brown eyes and soft lips and dark, artless curls appeared to him even more beautiful as they concentrated on the keyboard. Where did all that beauty and agility come from, he often wondered. The children were more lovely, more vital than he ever could have imagined them; they seemed at every moment poised upon a crossroads, dancing on their toes, arms open to the four winds. Bursts of happiness would fill him now and then on account of them, and he would seem to have been led to the center of a circle to dance with his daughters, with his wife, while all around them were music and patterns of light.

At the end of each lesson Carol Harper stood, the pupil stood, and they bowed to one another. Then Paul would exchange a few pleasantries with her and they would part until the following week. At home Paul would turn on lights, prepare a supper and then as usual see that the children fed the cat and helped with the dishwashing and practiced the piano, and then he would trudge upstairs behind them where they might play a game of cards or read a story aloud on the big bed. In their own rooms Kate sometimes sat at her desk, bent beside the lamp light; Marie might play with her blocks and dolls, accompanied by a sing-song monologue; Paul would then lie down for a few minutes with the evening paper or a book, before he got down to the always pressing business of serious studying.

His field was political science, and in the last few years he had put forth several articles on emerging forms of European cooperation that were bringing him the beginnings of a reputation. As he scanned the newspaper, his eyes would feel heavily lidded with the intensity of his intelligence. The book he hoped to write existed like a constant pressure behind his eyes; phrases hammered at his consciousness, unbidden—*shifting of attitudes, unusual flux, the continuum of development and decay*—, crying out to be brought under control. But was he ready? Did he know enough? Page after page he turned as he forced himself to stay awake and bring his mind to bear on more and yet more of the material of the world.

One midnight he woke dumbfounded to find his bedside light on, the newspaper fallen to his chest, himself still dressed, his throat very sore. Beside him the yellow cat lay curved in sleep on the pillow that should have been his wife's. Night had taken over entirely. Without him the children had put themselves in their own beds; unknown to him a new snow had whitened the dark, closing them even more deeply into winter. He went downstairs to lock the doors, and a translucent emptiness struck him to the heart. He telephoned his wife.

"Marta?"

"Paul!" she said, thick with sleep. "Darling, what time is it? Is everything all right?"

He could barely speak; he could barely swallow. He imagined the deep, open neckline of her nightgown as she propped herself up to talk and her dark, dishevelled hair and the way she would be reaching out to turn on the light and pick up her watch from among her books. He huddled over the telephone in the cold kitchen.

"Nothing is wrong," he said. "I love you."

Each time they paused, they were still connected. He could hear her breathing; he could almost hear her mind working and her heart beating. The silence after the call seemed irrationally absolute.

In the morning he woke feverish and dizzy. He guided himself from bathroom to bed, feeling unreal, and returned to sleep. When next he woke, he saw the face of Marie very close to his on the pillow, her eyes fixed on him. With an effort he came up through his sickness to meet her.

"I'm sick," he said.

"Daddy," she responded, naming him. She laid a hand on his chest.

"Will you get yourself some breakfast?" he asked. "I don't think we're going to make it to school today." There was a ringing between himself and his voice.

He watched the sympathy on her face turn into anticipation. "Can we watch TV?" she asked.

He nodded painfully, trying to joke. "Just don't make yourselves sick."

She dropped her head to his chest and hugged him briefly. "Daddy," she repeated happily, petting him, "get well, Daddy." Then she skipped out of the room.

He turned his face to the frost-rimmed window and the sunless view of the bared maple branches. He stared at the wallpaper, chosen neither by himself nor his wife, in which there were little faces to be found, repetitiously grimacing. There was one closet in the room and one cluttered bureau with a bleak, dusty mirror above it. There was no one to take care of him. He closed his eyes and sank beneath the ringing in his head to sleep.

Later in the morning he pulled himself up and dialed the secretary of his department to cancel his classes. He called the music school and left word that he would be unable to bring the girls in that afternoon. Oh, too bad! exclaimed the secretary, she hoped he would be better soon. Yes, he answered, it was probably just the flu. He hung up, took one look at his unshaven, haggard face and collapsed into the pillow.

The grimacing faces met his on every turn of his feverish head. His eyes saw distortion. At the grey window elongated tree branches stretched into a fantastic winter, while minute by minute he himself seemed to be contracting inside an unbelievable body. Fear clamped his chest and throat. It was barely possible to breathe, so great was the constriction. Helplessly he thumped the bed with his fist.

The children came through the doorway and stood side by side, still in their bedclothes, their hair unbrushed, looking down at him. "Bring me a bottle of mineral water, will you, Kate?" he asked. Marie continued to gaze at him silently. "You look funny," she finally pronounced. He closed his eyes and wished she would go away. The grip of disorder seemed permanent.

"I can't open the bottle," said Kate, returning to the bedside.

"Of course you can!" he said, suddenly angry, desperate.

"I've tried and I can't," she said. "Here," and she thrust the bottle and the opener towards him.

"I want you girls to go and turn off that television." He raised his voice hoarsely and watched surprise snap into their features. "Do you hear me? You've got to pull yourselves together and take care of things. I'm too sick to move."

They scurried away, and for a long time he lay breathing heavily and clutching the bottle to his chest. He thought about death. Finally he raised himself up, forced the cap from the bottle and took a long drink of the smooth, rounded water.

Then he waited. There was nothing else to do. All day time lost its standardization. Large wedges of hours might pass without his awareness, or moments be sliced into painful segments.

At dusk he heard the children quarrelling in another bedroom but felt too weak to interfere. Finally he called them in and asked them what they had eaten during the day.

"Now listen," he said with difficulty, and he told Kate to scramble some eggs. He wasn't sure what else there was to eat, but they could have toast and milk and some fruit and then they were to feed the cat and make sure all the lights were turned off and come upstairs and wash themselves for bed. Did she understand?

Kate nodded. "Will you be better tomorrow?" she asked.

"I'll still be sick tomorrow, but you girls are to get up and take the school bus. Today was an exception."

No, no, they protested, they wanted to stay home with him.

They weren't sick, were they? he asked anxiously. How did they feel?

Fine, they answered, except, yes, they were sick, and please, please couldn't they stay home with him? Kate sat down on the edge of the bed and Marie began to crawl under the covers with him.

"Ah, go away!" he exclaimed. "You're wearing me out." He gave Marie a little push, but she only pressed closer to him.

"Daddy," she said, nestling against him, her arm across his chest. Kate also lay alongside him, propped her head in her hand, and began to study him. She looked very much like Marta and also very much like his mother and his youngest sister.

"What have you been doing all day?" he asked.

"Everything," she answered. "I like to stay home better than I like to go to school."

"Oh, you do, do you?" he said neutrally. It was a great effort to respond. Kate dropped her head to his shoulder and the three of them lay still. It was nearly dark in the room. He closed his eyes.

"I read two library books this afternoon," murmured Kate.

"That's good," he answered without opening his eyes. He felt her adjusting the covers under his chin.

"Daddy, don't you just love unmade beds?"

"Is that where you've been reading?"

"I made a nest," she answered, "and I let Marie come in, too."

"Sometimes she did," corrected Marie, "but she kept the best pillows."

Invisibly, the wood inside the old bureau near the bed cracked and was quiet. The animate weight of his children rose and fell with his own difficult breaths. A faint, sudden current of released joy passed through him, almost too swiftly to be trusted; a heavy lid had lifted, a slit of light had appeared briefly along an inner horizon. All might be well; all might not be well.

"You've still got to go to school tomorrow, no matter how you feel about unmade beds," he said finally. "Now both of you hop out of here and go get yourselves some supper. Go on, out! out!" He elbowed them gently away, but then brought them in close embrace again. "Now take good care of each other," he whispered into their hair. They hugged him, and for a time the pressure of their arms lingered in the memory of his skin.

At night, however, when the children slept, he was absorbed so deeply into the topography of his illness that he felt lost from the touch of his daily life. The laws of this strange land were unknown. There were incalculable mountains to climb and troughs of dimensionless space to cross and narrow, extremely important places to shudder through. Humming voices and sinister elastic arms waited for him at every turn. On one smoking, crater-pocked plain a battle was being fought. For a long time he watched, as a traveller watches a scene onto which he has happened, but then he realized that the battle was his own; he was the principal. A figure came out of a crater to meet him, and as he tensed himself to face the advance, he wakened into the first light of another colorless winter day.

He was sicker than before. He scarcely heard the children preparing for school. When Kate brought in another bottle of water and a plate of toast, he thought wildly of asking her to stay home and nurse him, but then she seemed too much a child, too potentially demanding in her own right. Thanking her weakly, he closed his eyes again before she had even left his bedside.

He heard the front door closing and the voices of the children rising into the outside air. It sounded cold. He rolled his face against the pillow and drew up his knees. In between the rising and falling of intensities in his sickness, he listened dully to his labored breathing. He remembered Marta's breathing when the children were being born. Both births he had witnessed, and if there had been any way to take on part of the labor himself, he would have done it, he would have done anything. He had not been able to bear the thought of being left behind. She had seemed to be following a cord into an immemorial vitality. Marta, Marta, he had said when her eyes had closed and she had turned inward toward her enthralling pain, Marta, my dear.

He dreamt that he alone must enter a basement window, almost no more than a crack above the ground. It was necessary that he leave his briefcase underneath a sycamore tree. Hand it to me, will you? he implored the children when he finally accomplished his entry, but they did not seem to understand; they were laughing and dancing. All that work, please, please, he begged again, but his dry words went nowhere.

At noon, urinating, he rested his head against the cool wall beside the toilet. When he was back in bed and the dizziness had passed, he pulled the telephone next to his pillow and called his cleaning woman. She might be able to come today and bring groceries, he thought; perhaps she could even cook the children a meal.

"Sick are you?" said Mrs. McClentin. "And what might the trouble be?"

"The flu, I think. I should be on the mend by tomorrow."

"Now I don't know what to say," she said. "My grandchildren are coming on Saturday, as I told you, and what if I should be getting sick myself and not able to keep them? The flu is a terrible kind this year, they say, just terrible. I don't know but that I don't want to set foot in your door, if you understand my problem."

Ah, yes, he said, he did understand, but there was this matter of the groceries. He hung tightly to the receiver.

"You poor man," she said. "I'll tell you what, I'll pick up a few things later in the afternoon and come by with the bag and your Kate can take over from there."

That was kind of her, very kind, he said as he hung up.

He lay back dramatically, pitying himself, and looked at his watch. Two minutes had passed. Adjusting the time to Marta's zone, he imagined her walking freely down a street in her own local snow. Her back was to him; she did not know his needs. He narrowed his eyes at the sullen window square. Well-being to each person was a pressing daily matter; now, daily, he and Marta lived in ignorance of each other. And time was passing, month after month. Marta had gone her own way, all right. He thumped his fist angrily against the bed. Endless legions of wallpaper faces grimaced at him. Objects in the small room stood firm in their disarrangement. On the bureau there were books and papers, photographs, underwear, coins, Marie's toy monkey. HI DADDY, Kate had written into the dust of the mirror.

Shortly before the children were to come home from school, he forced himself to sit up and eat a piece of the cold toast. He drank a good deal more water and then set the empty bottle down, exhausted. The front door slammed, and another evening had begun. It was the second day. Wasn't it the second day? Or was it the third? He wondered where he would find the strength to continue.

They brought up the mail and piled it on his chest. There was one from Mommy, they shouted; he should open it, open it. Cold emanated from their clothing, drafts of cold stirred around his neck, his stomach knotted and turned. He swept aside the envelopes. The fingers of the children were icy. They were both talking at once. He didn't know how he was going to get through it. He wanted to disown them. The energy that was being sucked up from him was unbelievable. Their voices were high and excited.

"Go away," he said to them, and when they didn't respond, he barked, "get out of here!" and then nauseating blackness overwhelmed him, blackness with tiny speckles of red and far, far away voices, coming from the far end of a tunnel, a black tunnel, prickled with red.

Someone was wiping his mouth. "Not that way, this way!" said Kate's voice. "Here, you take the towel."

"I want Mommy," wailed Marie.

"Well, she's not here. Now help me with this sheet."

He lay in clammy stillness. His children were doing things to him. Kate was lifting his arm.

"Daddy, you've got to sit up."

"No," he said, "I can't."

"You've got to. Come on."

He sat up and they clumsily put a clean pajama top on him. His head fell back on a different pillow. A clean sheet was brought over his chest, then blankets.

Someone's child was crying.

"Stop that, Marie!" said Kate. "Come with me."

He heard water running in the bathroom and voices and feet hurrying down the stairs. He was floating away now, an empty, ringing shell of himself.

Something was being held to his ear. "Wake up," said Kate, pressing the hard telephone receiver against him. "Wake up. I called Mommy and she wants to talk to you."

"Paul? Shall I fly out? How bad are you?"

"I don't know," he said.

"I don't know what to do. I'm grading mid-terms. Have you seen a doctor?"

"No one," he answered.

"What are your symptoms?"

She made a sound of sympathy after each item. "Yes, well, two days, you said? Then you really should be out of it in a day or two. Oh God, this is awful. Are you remembering to drink?"

"I threw up."

"Then you've got to take smaller amounts. Let me talk to Kate."

Wordlessly he handed over the receiver.

It was amazing how empty he felt, how weightless, floating in a new elation of emptiness. Soon there would be nothing left of him. He felt quieter now, quiet and empty.

"Daddy, take a drink of water," said Kate.

"No, not yet."

"Mommy said you had to. She said for me to use this straw."

Marie climbed onto the bed and sat cross-legged beside his body. "I'm going to read you a story I wrote," she said when he had taken a swallow of water. "It's called Toby the Skunk. 'Once upon a time there was a skunk named Toby. He was naughty. He lived in a house with his mother and his father and his sister Emily. One day they went to a Chinese restaurant.' "

"Daddy, are you listening? You're supposed to stay awake and drink water."

There was a child sitting on either side of him. The cat had come to lie at the top of his pillow on the crown of his head. He took another sip of water.

" 'Toby wouldn't eat any of the Chinese food. Emily ate everything and so she got a fortune cookie. Toby didn't get anything.' "

"Is that the end?" he asked. "What happens to Toby?"

"That's all the farther I've gotten."

"Did you write that at school?"

"No, I wrote it in my room."

"I like your story," he said. "I want to hear the end of it." He licked his dry lips and felt the tired calm in his cheeks. "I think I should rest now. Why don't you both go downstairs and get something to eat? I'll be better now." He felt pleased to be so emptied of himself.

When their piano practicing began downstairs, he was half-asleep. Scales ascended and descended with falters and alignments until the rightful sequences were rediscovered. Structures of sound bore him aloft. Far below he heard Kate hesitatingly put together the hands of the Bach minuet, which until now she had been practicing separately. Yes, that's it, he encouraged her silently as the complexities were drawn into place. Nothing much existed now except the sheerness of himself and the music and his children. He felt satisfied by his illness.

The next morning after the children had left for school, he made his way downstairs for the first time and enjoyed the slight strangeness he found to the rooms. He would have liked to keep it. He wouldn't go too fast, he told himself, he would just do one thing at a time. He broke an egg into boiling water and set a piece of bread to toast. He looked out the kitchen window at the plain grey sky and the snow and the snow-lined spray of redbud branches. He carried the children's cereal bowls to the sink, rinsed out the milk and bits of cereal and wiped the table. In his deliberateness he nursed his slightly bouyant, quiet separateness. He was a vessel of untold value. When the egg was poached, he spooned it onto toast, set a fork and a napkin by his plate, and sprinkled a few grains of salt onto the filmed yolk.

Under the wall clock was a calendar at which he gazed as he slowly chewed: music lessons, a departmental meeting for himself, a piano recital for both girls the following Sunday. His eye slid easily along the squares of the week; maps were like that, too, the multicolored world yielding to a glance. He pressed up with his fork the last of the egg-soaked crumbs. Bite by bite everything that had been on his plate had been taken inside himself. The daylight in the kitchen was even more subdued; it would snow, perhaps, by evening.

Back in bed, he took up the stack of mail and found Marta's letter. With one hand as he read he stroked his three-day beard. Now and then he coughed deeply and drew the covers higher over his vulnerable chest. The letter had been written very early in the morning, after his midnight telephone call.

Dear Paul,

I haven't been able to go back to sleep yet, but I'm not uneasy any longer lying awake in the middle of the night. Will it seem strange to you if I say that I think I am learning at last how to live? I don't know why it should have taken something drastic like this year to help me come into this birthright, but so it has. Your call tonight—what really was on your mind? Do you know how often I think of you three there? What is happening to me is in spite of the ache of not being with you. In the classroom I think at last I am finding my own voice. I have this terrific sense of privacy. I walk around thinking, it's nobody else's damn business who I am or who I am becoming. Do you understand? I am happy to wake up every day. It was as if for a while I had forgotten how to speak.

I love you. I am taking long walks every weekend—last Sunday to the wharves. Excellence is on my mind. I am thinking of how the path might be kept clear.

I miss you all so much. I miss the sight of the children's bodies getting undressed for baths. Yours. The reality of what I'm not touching overwhelms me sometimes.

I had another letter from your mother last week, and it upset me greatly for a time, still does, I guess. She implies that I am way beyond my limits. She's worried about you, of course. I don't know how to answer her except in time.

Where would we be if you hadn't your wonderful ability to take the long view? You've steadied me many times. I wish I could tell you how deeply you have contributed to my sanity. I want to live *with* you. The future seems open. Tell me really

why you called. There has to be something you weren't saying.
I feel so right about this year and yet my mind is always half on
you because it has to be right for you, too.

Tell the girls I have gotten their Valentines and will write to
them tomorrow. And now I must sleep. I hope you are sleeping well. Kisses to you all.

My love,
Marta

Paul rolled onto his side towards the window. The long view: was
it true what she said? How strong was his mind? He fell asleep and
dreamt that he had an erection the length of his arm; it is as long as
my arm, he laughed to himself incredulously in the dream. It was the
most amazing erection he had ever had. He woke up laughing,
coughing, went to the bathroom, and came back to bed where he
slept peacefully until afternoon. It was snowing, without bluster,
when he woke.

That night Kate came into his bedroom to brush her hair by the
bureau mirror. She had recently taken an interest in her hair and
now stood in her nightgown, turning her face from side to side as she
gazed at herself and brushed. Paul watched her. At the beginning of
the winter term she had been weighed and measured by the school
nurse: four foot eleven and seventy-eight pounds, she had announced that evening at the dinner table.

She pursed her lips and held up a handful of curls. "Shall I get my
hair cut, Daddy?" she asked without turning around.

"No," he said. "I like it."

She frowned at herself and continued brushing. He watched the
thin shoulders and arms of the new generation at work beneath the
flannel gown.

"Well, do you want it cut?" he asked.

"Oh, I don't know!" she said impatiently and left the room.

A moment later she came back to stand in the doorway. "Are you
really getting better?" she asked.

"Yes, thank you," he answered, "much better. I think I'll get up
and start bossing you around tomorrow."

"Good," she sighed, "because everything is sure messed up around here."

All weekend indoors he wore the same old heavy sweater and navy blue knit hat and scarf. He drank hot lemonade with honey as he sat at his desk making notations in the margins of student research papers. Beneath his study in the basement the washing machine churned through its cycles. In the living room the girls had made a sprawling house of many rooms with their blocks, filled with scraps of cloth and carpet samples and empty thread spools. They came in occasionally to lounge against his chair. They toyed with his scarf and the curls of hair sticking out below his hat.

"Daddy," drawled Marie, testing his still unshaven cheek with her small hand, "come and play house with us."

"I am playing house with you." He made a large question mark in a margin and then looked up to smile at her.

"No, you're not, you're just doing your old work."

All weekend he watched the three of them living together, wrapped up in winter, a father and two daughters. He kept his eye on life from the vantage of his still tender, slowly improving condition.

"Play with us," his daughters begged him again.

With two columns and an arched block and two triangular blocks for an apex he made a second, grander doorway to their house.

"Not there," said Kate. "We've already got a door. Here, you can work these pieces."

He lay down on his side with his head in his hand, several wooden trucks and figures lined up in front of him, and mildly watched his children. In a little while they appeared not to need him.

Sunday afternoon he took another nap and woke feeling more rested than he had in a long time. He built a fire in the living room fireplace, spread a tablecloth on the floor as Marta sometimes used to do, and served a supper of toasted cheese sandwiches and fruit in the light of the flames. After he had cleared away the plates of apple parings, he lay down on the floor again and let the children wrestle with him. "More!" they shrieked. "More! Again!" His hat fell off, his scarf came loose and the ceiling and walls and floor were lambent with firelight. They wrestled until he lay back laughing and coughing and begging them to stop. The dancing patterns of light were beautiful. He lay flat on his back, breathless. It was as if he had just found himself to be there. "Let's tickle him again!" shouted Kate with a musical cascade of giggles.

On his return to work the next week, he continued to wear the heavy sweater and knit hat and scarf as badges of his nearly completed journey through the influenza. He had grown fond of the outfit. In the hallways he greeted his colleagues spiritedly. From the lecture platform he looked out into faces that were scarcely a decade older than those of his children. He listened to his own voice. Was he being clear? It seemed especially important that he be as articulate as he was able.

At noon he stayed in his office for a cup of bouillon and the sandwich he had brought from home. He took his lunch to the window and sat on the broad sill with a lookout over the university and the church spires to the end of town, where rolling fields of snow began. Squinting through the steam of his cup into the noonday light, he could almost see how this new world must at first have appeared. Now small planes tilted, glinting, down out of the sky towards the small airport where once uncut grasses and jack rabbits had abounded. He had glimmers of newly discovered territories in himself that he wondered how to keep sight of.

The children as usual took the bus home from school, let themselves in the back door with their own key, and then called him at his office to say they had arrived. On Monday he left early to shop for food and that night cooked a real dinner and felt energetic enough to put in several hours of evening reading after the children were asleep. His cough was much better. At ten-thirty he stopped, so as to be sure he got enough sleep, took a shower, put on his pajamas, and with the feeling that a successful day was coming to a close, he stepped into the concentrated hush of the children's bedrooms. Sitting for a few minutes on each of the beds, he could feel his breathing slow toward their sleeping breaths; he could feel their presence entering and filling his heart. Beneath tacked up pictures of horses and dogs and panda bears, Marie lay flung out inside the motion of a dream. He watched her sealed eyes, her parted lips, her round cheeks and then he covered her and crossed to Kate's room. The cat looked up from the bed and yawned. It was the room of a child almost no longer a child. Knowledge seemed to be appearing in the new angularity of her body and the planes of her face. In nine years she would be the age Marta had been when they had met. He reached out a hand to smooth back her hair, but as she at that moment stirred, sighed and curled more deeply into sleep, he gave the cat a scratch instead and returned to his own room, happy.

On Wednesday, detained by a student, he closed his office at four-fifteen and hurried home through the fading light to pick up the girls for their piano lessons.

He found them lying feet to feet on the couch reading comic books.

"Come on!" he said. "I expect you to be ready by the time I get here. You're old enough to keep track of the time."

Marie stretched indolently; Kate continued to read, twirling a dark curl of hair around her finger.

Paul strode across the room and jerked the cheap paper from her hands. Kate grinned up beautifully, winningly.

"Kathryn," he made himself roar. "Get your shoes on! You, Marie, shoes! jacket! Quick!" He clapped his hands, urgent in his wish to inspire. His children were like lumps. They shivered and complained and poked each other in the car. Why couldn't they just stay home and read, they wanted to know. It was too cold for piano lessons today.

"Hush," he said to them, keeping his vision attentive to what was ahead. He parked the car and herded them along the icy sidewalk and up the steps of the music school.

The secretary looked up from a file box. A violin was being tuned somewhere. The waiting room was empty. "We're late," Paul said to Marie. "We'll go straight on up." Kate collapsed into the corner of the couch to wait her turn and opened one of the comics she had brought along with her music.

"Miss Harper is upstairs?" Paul asked the secretary.

"She should be," answered the secretary. "She stepped down a few minutes ago to see if you had come."

He and Marie clomped noisily up the wooden stairs to the

deserted auditorium, which was faintly lit by the twilight in the tall, arched windows. Old-fashioned chandeliers of fluted, flower-like glass bells hung at intervals over the two hundred empty seats, and a stencilled design ran along the upper edge of the painted walls where the wooden ceiling slanted up. It was a charming, intimate hall.

"Hush, wait," said Paul, staying Marie with his hand on her shoulder.

"What for?"

"Listen!"

In the stillness they heard the piano music, not the stumblings of a child's lesson in progress, but liquid repetitions of a difficult phrase, then the passage to which it belonged, itself repeated, then repeated again, the musicality of the touch so astonishing that Paul stood without moving. Again the difficult phrase was extracted for attention; a comprehensive mind was at work; there was a mistake, a recovery, another attack; notes poured out cohesively, assuredly. It sounded nearly perfect to Paul. Hesitantly he continued up the stairs. The door was closed to the small room beside the stage. As they crossed the platform to it, he could hear human sounds along with the music, humming, a groan, sniffing. "Ah!" said the voice in exasperation at the poised apex of a crescendo. The music broke off abruptly and two hands landed hard on a dissonant chord.

Paul knocked softly. There was a scraping within and the door was flung open by Carol Harper, her eyes shining with tears. "Well, you're here," she said in her quick voice. "Good. I thought you might still be sick."

"I enjoyed your playing just now," said Paul.

Carol gave a short laugh. "I'm out of practice, I'm afraid, terribly out of practice."

Paul took his chair, shed his jacket, and opened his notebook. Marie had slid onto the piano stool and was looking down at her boots, her shoulders hunched. Carol stood with her back to them in the curve of the piano's wing. She fumbled in her purse. She blew her nose. Sycamore branches and the shadows of sycamore branches moved within the arch of the window.

Carol turned around and shook back her hair. Her eyes were red. "Excuse me, please." She closed her eyes for an instant and seemed to be collecting herself. "Excuse me, I used to be able to play that piece, but I'm finding myself far rustier than I had realized."

Paul nodded sympathetically. Marie continued to look at her boots.

"Fifty-two students," enunciated Carol, her fist resting on the top of the piano, "I have fifty-two students."

Paul nodded again.

Then a slight tremor seemed to pass, cleansingly, through the young woman's body and her manner shifted. She quickly took her chair and clapped Marie on the shoulder with a friendly hand.

"Well, Marie, let's see what you're going to do today. Start with the scale, please, A major. Good. Now, left hand. All right, now can you tell me what the next scale will be?"

Paul wrote *scale* in the assignment book. Marie counted up the keyboard and then looked at her teacher with large eyes. Two adults waited for her pronouncement; a child was to carry forward the knowledge of the circle of fifths.

"E major?" asked Marie.

"Of course," said Carol. "Very good. Now would you try it, please? How many sharps does it have?"

Paul wrote *E major* in the notebook and took a deep, quiet breath as he settled into the lessons. His gaze travelled between Carol's earnest profile, the soft faces of his children, and the framed view of the winter, which intensified into an evening blue, and then by degrees as the color drained away the sycamore tree merged with the world. They were in a warmed cave of light.

Where did Carol live, Paul wondered. When did she find time to practice? Did she come here, to this room, during odd, deserted hours, or did she have an upright piano in her apartment, with a lamp on it and stacks of music and a bust of Shubert or Chopin or Beethoven? The simplicity of her dress, the directness of her speech, the intentness of her manner suggested economy, efficiency, a self subsumed into its purpose; but then there was this matter of the tears, the fear of not measuring up, the dissonance of struggle. His meditations stirred in him a deep layer of understanding.

Kate now was on the stool, looking drowsy and placid, her hair curling over her cheek. *Excellence is on my mind,* Marta had written. Kate played through her scale and her recital piece for Sunday, and then she tipped her head to one side and started in on the Bach minuet. As the music began to draw her in, she seemed to suck in on her cheeks; her eyes widened a little and her nose flared as she came to the difficult places. Paul saw himself in her expression, Marta in her eyes, her hair, his own mother, his sisters in the angle of her nose.

"Good," said Carol, who seemed recollected now from her agitation. "You've made a good start in putting the hands together. Now, this is a dance." She reached over and played the opening phrase. "The dancers need a strong beginning. Now you try. Yes, that's it, even more, right hand sing out, continue."

Paul stared at the pattern he saw emerging from the scene: those who were young and still searching for their own power, like himself, like Carol Harper, like Marta far away, yet cared for those even younger, lives unfolding out of lives, out of life, every moment pressing them onward. He was discovering himself to be already deep inside this pattern; it surrounded him like a dance, and what was important was the power between the dancers. He felt his heart reaching out, his mind stretching. Everything his finely trained intellect loved was still within his grasp—all those maps he was so fond of studying, with the red faction, the blue coalition, the green uncertainty about borderlines; all those political tendencies in crude slow motion shifting endlessly; all those theories, pleasing in their subtlety, researched, annotated, set down upon pages—but now he knew without doubt that he had also given himself over to a huge, whirling harmony, from which pattern within pattern could emerge. Sitting lightly in his chair, very still, he felt himself expanding to accept this vast motion, kindred to himself.

"I'll show you what the next part sounds like," said Carol to Kate. She stood up, reached her arms around the child to the piano and began a softer singing of the hands to one another, while Kate bowed slightly forward inside the enclosure of her teacher's body. "G minor," said Carol's voice above the music, "a trio, and now we return to the first minuet." After several measures she stopped and rested her hands on Kate's shoulders. "I think you'll enjoy putting all this together."

There were five minutes more to the lesson during which Carol heard Kate begin to read the separate hands of the new trio. "Very good," she concluded, "You'll have plenty to do this week." She and Kate bowed to one another and then she stood aside by the door.

"Thank you," said Paul, standing, a body in a down jacket, a mind full of waves of appreciation for this teacher, for Bach, for the small room inside the dusk, for the germinal presence of Kate.

"When we came up the stairs and heard you playing, I did think it sounded wonderful," he went on to Carol, as Kate began to gather up her music and jacket.

"Well, thank you," she answered, "but I haven't had nearly the time I need for practicing lately. I must make some decisions about this—and soon."

"Do you want to perform?"

"Basically I want to write about music. But I want to play very well, and of course I want students, too." She looked at Kate affectionately. "I'll be going back to school before long, as soon as I've saved a bit more money."

Paul nodded. Kate stood ready in her hooded jacket. It was five-thirty. Another student, a thin blond boy of about ten whom they passed each week, would be waiting with Marie in the office downstairs. Kate pulled on her father's hand.

"So," said Paul. "The recital on Sunday is at two?"

"Two o'clock, barring a blizzard or the end of the world," said Carol gaily.

On the way home both girls sat beside him in the front seat of the car. "Daddy, what did Carol mean by the end of the world?" asked Kate.

"She was making a joke."

"Is the world going to end?"

"No one knows."

Kate was silent. At bedtime she asked, "Then what would happen if the world ended?"

"No one knows that either."

"Well, you and me and Marie are going to stay in this house, and Mommy's coming home, and we're not going to move again."

"Is that the way it's going to be?" He bent close to her face and pulled the pillow up around her ears.

"Yes," she said definitively. "I say so."

"I'm with you," he said, kissing her in the center of her forehead.

For several hours after the children were in bed he sat reading in the deep chair beside his desk, settled down inside the sounds of his house. He had put on his knit hat again and wrapped an old blanket around his shoulders. As he read, he made a number of notations; he could feel material massing behind his eyes. He read of burgeoning international organizations. Where was the power to be? Who could foretell a future map of the surface of the earth? Page after page of facts and theories were being folded into his mind. Signs of evolution were what he was watching for, expressions of deep-rooted economy; for it was, he knew now, only beneath a broad aspect of orderliness that he wanted to organize the wealth of his studies.

On Sunday morning, which was cold and bright and full of winter birds and sharp, bluish shadows on the snow, all three of them took baths, first Paul and then, while he cooked breakfast, both the girls, squealing, together.

"Pancakes in five minutes," he shouted up the stairwell.

They thudded down to the kitchen, giggling, scrubbed, claiming to be too nervous about their recital to eat a bite.

"Start with one," said Paul as he set down a pitcher of hot maple syrup. The girls each ate four cakes, a banana and a glass of milk. "That should hold you," said Paul with satisfaction. All the while they had been eating he had delighted in the sunshine on their hair and the delicate flush on their cheeks and the ceaseless play of their talk.

"Hold me *down,*" said Kate. "I won't be able to climb on stage." She gripped her stomach, rolled her eyes at him and laughed.

By five minutes before two, twenty-eight children had taken their places on the long bench beneath the tall windows of the auditorium, a shining human strand of barely containable energy. Adults, more accustomed to the surgings of life, maintained characteristic composures. Carol and several other teachers walked up and down the row, now and then bending low to speak to a child.

Paul greeted the father next to him, a Japanese of about his own age, who made several more adjustments to his camera before lowering it in readiness to his lap.

"Which child is yours?" the man asked, indicating the children.

"That little girl in the blue dress, third from the end, and the one in brown in the center," said Paul.

"Ah, beautiful children, beautiful. Mine there, boy in red and girl with violin." He nodded his head in pleasure.

"Yes, I see them," said Paul and then he added ceremoniously, "your children are also beautiful."

"Ah, thank you," said the Japanese father, his face melting into a sweet, full, happy smile, "thank you."

The Lap of Peace

It is the end of the morning, a hot Saturday in June. Richard and Claire are having an argument, of sorts. Now there is a breathing spell. Claire, seven months pregnant with their second child, is dozing in a rickety lounge chair on the unweeded terrace. Nearby, beneath a blooming mock orange bush, Jeffrey squats over a cluster of ladybugs, stick in hand. Richard, having showered after a four-mile jog out of town and back along the county road, steps to the open bathroom window to towel down his young, healthy body and beholds his wife and his three-year-old son below, on the verge of the tangled yard, a still life in the midst of a thicket of unfinished projects. Breasts and belly rest in the curve of Claire's body like fruits in a basket; her arm dangles; her head is tipped to one side.

The primary matter of the argument has been the ninety-year-old, unfurbished house and its ten acres, which run back from terrace and garden and half-dead orchard through timber choked by multiflora rose down to a muddy creek. It has turned out to be an exceedingly difficult bit of heaven, purchased for a song last October when the countryside was yielding up warm, inspiring color, camped out in with both grimness and gaiety through the winter months, and now forcing upon their human wits unreckoned fecundity and dilapidation.

Richard's ambitious vision includes a windmill, insulation, sanded floors, tuck-pointing, fresh paint, new kitchen and bathroom fixtures, tidied gardens and orchard, well-managed wood lot, teeming creek. . . . Claire has only lately begun to admit her growing fondness for the walls just as they are, time-marked with brown stains, faded wallpaper and lichenlike plaster, in whose humble depths she sometimes fancies another order can be found. Outside, she has planted a few seeds, some of them secretly, but she would like the wildness to remain, at least for a time. . . .

Richard puts on his work clothes and thuds energetically down the stairs and through the sparely furnished rooms to the terrace.

"Daddy," says Jeffrey, jumping up, "come and see the bugs."

"Where's that?"

"My house." The boy takes his hand and pulls him to the bush. The unpruned branches catch in Richard's hair as he bends down to the matting of leaves and stirred-up insects.

"Come in all the way."

"I want to talk to Claire."

"She sleeping."

"I think she's pretending. Shall I see if she's pretending?"

Perspiration has collected beneath the boy's wide-open eyes. He begins to suck his thumb.

Richard creeps across the brick terrace, sits at the base of the lounge chair and reaches up to stroke Claire's right foot.

"Hello, Richard," says Claire without opening her eyes.

"Look at it this way," says Richard. "If we get that south room done in time for my parents, then it will be all set for the new nursery. Two birds with one stone."

"That's exactly what you said last night."

"Did I? I've forgotten all the things I said last night."

The secondary matter, but also the catalyst of the argument has been the impending and unusual visit of Richard's parents. Certain minimum standards of domestic comfort and refinement have to Richard's mind suddenly become more pressing than ever. He does not understand why Claire is not moving more rapidly towards what he thought was their common plan. Surely by this time the nesting instinct should be raving within her; he had been banking on it. Perhaps there is something to be worried about—laziness? malaise?

With the tips of his fingers he presses up and down along the delicate bones of her foot.

"How are you feeling?" he asks.

"All right."

"Don't you think it would be good if you moved around a little this morning?"

"And stripped a little wallpaper maybe?"

"Yes, all right, and stripped a little wallpaper."

"I was thinking a walk might feel good. Would you like to take a walk?"

"I just got back from jogging."

"Ah, so you did." Heavily, Claire plumps onto her side, away from him, and pulls her foot out from under his hand. Opening her eyes just a slit, she sees nothing but the dense greenery of the vegetative middle distance. The green is like the inevitable tunnel of birth into which she must go, all alone, like the rabbit she saw yesterday on the edge of the timber, bounding and disappearing into the multiflora rose.

"But maybe we could walk together later, when it's not so hot," says Richard.

Jeffrey comes to the lounge chair with two fistfuls of leaves and twigs, which he places on the skirt of Claire's sundress. "I make stew now," he says.

"All right," says Claire. "But you need some carrots, too. Go find some carrots."

"These are carrots," says Jeffrey.

"Then go find turnips. For this stew you definitely need some turnips."

Richard looks at his watch. He has rented a wallpaper steamer at a rate of forty dollars for the weekend. He thought they had agreed upon this project, at this particular time.

"Did you have some protein this morning?" he asks.

"Yes, I had some protein this morning," she mimicks.

"Do you want me to fix up this place single-handedly? Is that what you're saying?"

"I haven't said that."

"We have two weeks until they get here. The baby is coming.

Winter is coming. I absolutely do not understand how you can want to spend another winter like the last one."

"Neither do I."

Softening, Richard lays his hand on her raised hip. The material of her dress is light blue cotton, and it falls loosely from the mounded horizon of her body. On the periphery of his vision his son is approaching from the bushes with laden hands.

"What's that you're saying?" he asks Claire. "I can't hear you." He moves to the other side of the lounge chair and hunkers close to her face. How lovely and smooth she looks! Only a few years ago he had no knowledge of her. There he had been, out ramming around the world, his emotions spinning off in all directions at once, nothing to hold on to. "What did you say?" he repeats gently. He tries to position his face within the gaze of her half-closed eyes. Her breath touches him.

"Oh, Claire," he bursts out, "believe me, I would much rather live with you than without you."

She opens her eyes and regards him, he cannot tell with what expression.

Jeffrey has flung himself on the foot of the chair.

"What time is it anyway?" asks Claire.

"Almost noon."

"How would you like to take Jeffrey in and give him some lunch and put him down for his nap?" She raises an eyebrow at Richard.

Habitually, he looks again at his watch. From overhead he can feel the slow, arching advance of the sun. He feels cramped and hot. Claire's dress is the color of a smooth lake on a fine day.

"No, no, no," says Jeffrey, "no nap. I want stew."

"Did you find turnips?" asks Claire.

He clings to her leg and begins to cry.

"All right, all right," says Richard abruptly. With difficulty he detaches the struggling child and swings him up into his arms. "Ho! Now I've got you."

"No nap, no nap," screams Jeffrey. "I want Mama."

"It's me you've got," says Richard as he starts towards the house.

"Now don't forget to give him some protein," sings out Claire. She hears the screen door banging shut and then she brushes off all the twigs and sticky leaves from her skirt and legs. She lies back with a sigh. The baby pushes deep into her groin and hard up against her ribs. On the surface nothing appears to be happening. When she closes her eyes and lets her mind go to these inner movements, then she can make room for them more easily. She breathes deeply and slowly. She feels completely occupied. The terrace at last is quiet.

What is so rare as a day in June? Burdock is strangling the raspberry canes; deadly nightshade has overtaken the yew; Virginia creeper edges in from the timber; rabbits early this very morning nibbled off every new shoot from the row of bush beans. Between the bricks of the house mortar crumbles; gutters are choked with pigeon nests; an unpainted shed, taken over by wasps, sags beyond repair. The day drones and sings, incomparably sweetened by blossoms. Overhead there is no end to sky. Down by the creek iridescent dragonflies dart in sexual conjunction above ragwort and pink fern-leafed yarrow.

Upstairs in his crib, Jeffrey is sucking his thumb. There are some wonderful, bobbing shadows on the blank wall across the room, at which he stares, rocking his body, until his eyelids flutter, and the bobbing, rocking, patterned enclosure of the room dissolves into a gentle, inward oscillation. His hand falls away from his mouth; he sighs. He ate a good lunch of toasted cheese sandwich and apple slices and milk, and it is a satisfaction to Richard, now in the adjoining room struggling with the wallpaper steamer, to have watched his son sitting up sturdily in his new youth chair and eating a good lunch. That much went well enough. The clincher was when Richard snapped open his pocket knife and trimmed the peel from the apple into one perfect red helix above Jeffrey's outstretched palm. Friends again, they climbed unhurriedly up the wooden hill to bed.

But from the moment of closing the nursery door, Richard has again been seized within the vise of inner and outer necessity. It is not just that there are a tremendous number of things to do: he feels a tremendous need to improve his little territory. Each day he wants to move ahead. How else will he be able to see the force and direction of his own thought?

The steamer, however, is heavy and doesn't seem to be operating well. It steams unevenly, and water drips down the wand and along his arm. What a job! He turns off the machine and begins to scrape. Five layers of old paper there are. Underneath, the plaster is ancient. Covering up the whole mess with new plaster board might be a solution, but then they—he?—would run into depth problems with the ceiling and baseboard moldings, to say nothing of the window and door frames. It is hot in the room, even with the windows open. What he needs is an old-time plasterer to come in and give him a hand. First, though, there would still be this problem of the wallpaper, to be solved inch by inch. Another pair of hands would help, that's for sure. Richard takes off his shirt and shoes and rolls up his ragged jeans. Robinson Crusoe never had to worry about wallpaper, but then of course he had other things to worry about.

Richard drops his scraper onto a pile of shavings and goes down the hallway to the bathroom. Claire is no longer down below on the lounge chair, and he hears no sound of her in the house, either. Then his listening is covered over by the reverberating passage of an unseen number of motorcycles along the blacktop road on the other side of the house. Left in the wake of this slicing roar, he reminds himself that it is summertime, a Saturday afternoon of the finest texture, which people of all kinds, in all sorts of ways, set out to penetrate.

His helpmeet, had he searched for and found her, would not have wished at that moment to have been found by him. Sitting crosslegged against the far side of one of the old apple trees, close to the timber undergrowth, she is ostensibly eating a very large sandwich of avocado and tomato slices, alfalfa sprouts and Swiss cheese, but what she is really doing is practicing being alone with Mother Nature. A green vortex beckons between the trees ahead. Claire chews steadily, batting all the while at the annoying gnats that keep making for the corners of her eyes. The day has already slipped past its zenith. Claire narrows her eyes. Beyond this shimmering, motion-filled green she knows there will be snow. Storms from the northeast will crack off more apple limbs. One day she herself will be an old woman. It burdens her that she feels so ignorant now, and she does not know if her life, left to itself, will be able to teach her what she needs. A curious dream she sometimes has, of being in a white ceremonious city, with terraces and balustrades, beside a wide sea.

Now she is finished eating. She wipes her hands on the coarse grass and leans back against the tree, thrusting out her legs. Close to the digesting sandwich, the baby performs several enormous turns. Claire is thirsty. She has forgotten to bring along something to drink. Soon she will have no choice but to heave herself up and return. She thinks of Richard, alone in a room with a wallpaper steamer. She sighs. Why does she feel she must resist him? People live inside walls; she knows this. They marry, beget children, grow old embedded in cultures; these facts she does not feel she is shirking. And yet, her life being her own, the questions remain.

Nowadays Jeffrey usually doesn't cry when he first wakes up. Sometimes he sings, sometimes he sucks his thumb, sometimes he talks to his stuffed animals. Ever since he climbed over the top of his crib several months ago, the movable side has been kept lowered. There is a new bed across the room, and above this bed the shadows are still there. Jeffrey lets himself down from the crib, crosses the room, and pulls himself up onto the quilt of the new bed. He runs the palm of his hand over the shadows, he traces their shapes. Then he slides down from the bed, gets his shoe box of crayons, climbs back up onto the colorful quilt and begins to draw vigorously on top of the shadow patterns.

"Oh, dear, what's that you're doing?" says Claire. Her son is naked except for his underpants, and he is standing up, coloring with large motions as high as his arm will go.

"Clown and bees," says Jeffrey, "inside balloon, and then here come ladybugs!"

"Jeffrey, you're drawing on the wall. Are you supposed to do that?"

He drops his arm and looks at her.

"Crayon marks are very hard to clean up," says Claire, crossing the room. "Oh my goodness, you've made lots of them." She shakes her head, then peers with interest at the circular shapes. "Is this the balloon?"

"No, this one."

Sure enough, there inside is a semblance of a face and some small, intense marks.

"How did everybody get inside that balloon?"

"They live there. Here come ladybugs now." Jeffrey loses his guilty look and goes dot, dot, dot across the wall with his crayon.

"What about a bush?" asks Claire. "Do you need a bush?"

"A big bush."

Claire selects her colors with the mock orange in mind and kneels cumbersomely on the bed and begins with free sweeps of her hand to draw an arching spray of branches. Then she indicates a ground line of grass and below it, as she often did as a child, a downward-reaching network of roots. "Your bugs can come down here to sleep," she says to Jeffrey. She draws several little tunnels from the surface of the earth down to the network of roots and in them some antlike bugs. Everything she draws seems familiar to her, home territory.

After some moments of watching his mother, Jeffrey is now continuing spiritedly and noisily with his own drawing.

"Ye gods!" says Richard from the doorway. "I don't believe it." The toil of the last hour gives a ringing force to his voice. "Claire, do you know what you're doing?"

"Hello, Richard," says Claire. "The work was already well underway by the time I got here."

"But this is downright irresponsible. What do you think you're teaching Jeffrey?"

She colors one last yellow center on a mock orange blossom and sits down on the bed. She looks at Jeffrey and then at Richard. Jeffrey stands holding his crotch and looking at both of them. Richard is having one of those vertiginous moments when life seems forever and forever unorganizable.

"I don't know what I'm teaching Jeffrey," says Claire.

Jeffrey begins to let the pee out. Down goes the warmth and up goes his relief.

"Hold everything," shouts Richard. He swoops his son off the bed and carries him, dribbling, at arm's length down the hallway to the bathroom where he stands him in the bathtub. "I suppose you're all done," says Richard.

Jeffrey nods.

"Anything left?"

Jeffrey shakes his head.

"Well . . . ," says Richard, studying his son, flesh of his flesh.

Claire is following down the hall, pushing a diaper over Jeffrey's trail with her foot.

"Well," says Richard, looking up at her, bare legs, blue dress, knotted-up hair, "I suppose there's nothing to do but spray him off."

"That's a good idea," she agrees. "It's so hot anyway. Then maybe what we should do is just go down to the creek for awhile and get out of this house. Please?"

"Claire," says Richard. "Do you think that if you and I were to sit down and talk this house thing through from the beginning we could come to an end of it?"

"I don't know," says Claire, "but that might be better than what's going on now."

In the rudimentary kitchen Richard fills a canteen with water, and Claire washes a pint basket of strawberries and sets them in a bag. "Come here once," she says to Jeffrey and dabs some vanilla on the skin around his eyes. "You, too," she says to Richard, reaching up. "The gnats are horrendous out there."

"Is that where you were all that time?" he asks. His hands are on her swollen waist.

When they are ready to go, Richard stops off in the garage for some work gloves and a machete. Once in the timber he leads the way, hacking and yanking at the thickets of multiflora rose or holding aside handfuls of the arching, prickly stem tips so that his wife and son can pass. Claire carries the bag of strawberries in one hand and helps Jeffrey over fallen tree trunks with the other. Richard cuts and yanks and sweats, enjoying himself. Twice rabbits bound out from under bushes and clear spaces to safety with only a few of the swiftest, lightest hops.

"They disappear almost before you can think about them," says Claire as she sits down on a log and lifts her legs over.

The brambles stop at the open, grassy floodplain of the creek. Claire pinches off a leaf and holds it under her nose. "Bergamot," she says, "a nice big patch coming."

"Look how last year's grass is still flattened from the water," says Richard, poking at it with his machete. "It's amazing how the new can push up through all that."

Now Jeffrey has seen the water, and there is no stopping him. "We might as well go sit under the willow and let him play in the mud," says Claire.

The willow juts at an angle over an outer curve of the meandering creek. Exposed roots in the side of the bank provide foot- and hand-holds to help Jeffrey climb the short way down to the flat mud. For a few minutes he simply walks barefoot up and down the narrow strip of land, watching his footprints fill with water. Almost within his reach, a dragonfly hovers for an instant before skimming across the water. Jeffrey picks up one stone and then another and another. Claire looks down on him from the edge of the bank. He has begun to talk to himself. His toes curl into the mud with each step.

Richard takes off his belt with its canteen and knife and leans back against the tree. "Come on over here," he says to Claire.

She stays where she is a few minutes longer, arms crisscrossed on her chest, and then she comes and lies down on the grass with her head in his lap. "Don't you dare take your eyes off that child," she says. Above them the slender willow leaves shine like a shower of green and white light. Claire thinks that she will wait for Richard to begin speaking, but it is her own voice that says, "Why don't we just put some wallpaper up in Jeffrey's room and be done with it?"

"I hate wallpaper," says Richard. "Anyway, the crayon grease would still have to come off."

"Your mother has lots of wallpaper in her house."

"I know. I look at it for five minutes, and I'm already sick of it."

Claire lifts up Richard's left hand and places it on her navel where a baby heel or elbow or fist is thudding. He slides his hand around and around the softly-clothed womb.

"One trouble is," says Claire, "that I wish your mother weren't coming here when I'm pregnant."

"Are you too tired?"

She shrugs. "I'd just rather be alone with you, that's all. Your mother is so civilized."

"What's uncivilized about having a baby?"

She shrugs again.

Beneath his hand he senses in her so much life that a surge of expectation and well-being rises in his own body. "What are you talking about?'' He smiles down at her in a friendly way.

"Why is it necessary to put so much effort into things?" she bursts out.

"Do you like that house the way it is?" he asks.

"It's growing on me."

"It will disintegrate around you one of these days."

She sighs. "I think I'm really an eccentric old woman in disguise, getting ready to die."

Richard laughs outright.

Claire sits up and says loudly, "Doesn't it ever occur to you that what we're doing makes no sense? That we're wearing ourselves out for absolutely no reason at all?" She rips a handful of leaves from a drooping branch and begins to tear them apart.

Richard looks at her judiciously and then turns his gaze to Jeffrey, who is carrying large handfuls of mud from the water's edge to a project Richard can't see, just below the bank. He says nothing to Claire.

"I've never in my life been a lazy person," she continues. "I'm a good worker. I get good results."

"Would you please stop throwing leaves around and come sit next to me?"

"Richard, I think maybe we made a mistake buying this old place."

"Maybe we did. This doesn't have to be the end of the line."

"People say that," says Claire as she pulls at the grasses between them. "People say that, but they dig in anyway, and they get overwhelmed and forget what they ever thought about in the first place."

"I don't see how it helps not to dig in," says Richard. "I mean, this is where we're living. Don't you want things to be nicer?" He has taken the machete out of its sheath and is turning the blade this way and that so that it catches the light. "You don't sound like yourself," he adds. "You don't sound like an expectant mother."

She gets up and leaves him. She goes a short way down the bank and sits with her legs swinging over the edge.

Delighted, Jeffrey comes up to her toes with muddy hands. She lifts her feet above his head. "What are you making, Jeffrey?" she asks. He continues to reach for her feet; his giggles are like water rising up in the air and showering back down. "Come on," she laughs, "leave my feet alone and tell me what you're making."

"Come down and play."

"No," says Claire. "I'm going to stay right here and watch you. Show me how you do it."

Jeffrey crouches at the edge of the water, knees on either side of his head, to scoop up more mud.

"I'm sorry," says Richard, coming over to her. "Tell me what I said."

She squints across the creek at the plant life on the opposite bank. "Richard," she says finally, "sometimes I have this dream about being in a white city. What do you think that means?"

"Why a white city?"

"That's what I'm asking you."

"Maybe a past life," he says.

Claire looks at his lean, healthy face. She remembers that ever since rising this morning he has been purposively in action: exercises in the sunlight, a nutritious breakfast, an hour of reading, some garden work, a long run away from the house, the feeding of his son, wallpaper stripping and, of course, these discussions with his wife. How accomplished, how organized, how flexible he is! His posture is graceful, of contained vitality, like that of a young burnished god momentarily at ease.

She bites her lips and continues to study him.

"Well?" he asks.

"Richard, what were we thinking about when we bought this place?"

"Peace and quiet. A corner of earth. A year ago all we had was a dirty balcony—do you want me to remind you of exactly how it was?"

"No," she says, lowering her head over her interlaced fingers.

She begins again. "We're not starving, we're not political prisoners, we're not trying to escape across the mountains or the sea. We're fortunate." She pauses. "I would like to know what to do with that." She sends him a sideways look.

Richard unfolds his legs and inches closer to her; he circles her middle with his arms; he kisses her cheek just in front of her ear where a tendril of hair has loosened. "I'm glad we're not trekking over a mountain just now," he says.

Claire raises her hands to her face. "I would walk anywhere if I thought I could find out what I need to know," she says dramatically. She turns to face him. "Honestly I would."

For a moment alarm shoots through Richard. His arms are full of he knows not what. He lowers his forehead to her shoulder. "I think," he says carefully, "that what we should do is to have this baby and then see what happens."

"Right now I'm having a déjà vu," she says.

"Claire, I think attitude is extremely important."

She says nothing.

"Look here," he begins, then is silent. He straightens his spine; he stretches up his strong arms until his fingertips tingle; he shakes himself loose. How well, how capable he feels! He gets up and comes back with the strawberries. "Jeffrey," he calls, "wash off your hands and come up and have a strawberry."

Jeffrey stops a moment and looks up at them, mucky hands dangling. "No," he says.

"Listen to that," says Richard, handing Claire a strawberry. "He's stubborn."

"Just like his father."

"Just like his mother," says Richard amicably. He begins to eat. The strawberries have an excellent flavor. He selects another one for her, the best he can find. This argument of theirs does not seem so very serious, really. When the water gets too deep, well, then, you just float back to shore for awhile. It's simple. And the day is so fine. Claire is right: the house mustn't encroach on their pleasure in each other. "Good idea you had, coming here," he says with his mouth full.

"Richard," she says, "what I'm talking about is very serious."

He nods. "I haven't stopped thinking." He holds another strawberry in front of her, in the palm of his hand.

"By the way," he says, "I found some interesting sprouts along the northeast fence this morning. Sunflowers maybe. Could they have seeded themselves down?"

"I planted those," says Claire.

Dusk comes that night by such subtle gradations that it would be impossible to choose a moment when the close-knit day is taken over by the far-flung night. Jeffrey offers no resistance to being bathed and fed and tucked into bed.

"What about our picture on the wall?" whispers Claire as she leans over the crib. "Shall we wash it off tomorrow?"

Jeffrey shakes his head, no. His thumb is in his mouth, his eyes are nearly closed.

Claire smiles, in spite of herself. She pulls the tops of his pajamas down over his round stomach. "Do you know what a bulletin board is?" she asks. "We could put a big one on the wall and you could pin up all your drawings—would you like that? Or a blackboard, so that you could draw with chalk?"

But he is too nearly asleep to answer. She stands beside the bed.

"Asleep?" asks Richard, coming in.

"Look how long he is, Richard," she whispers. "I think he's going to be taller than you."

"Like Uncle Bill."

"Or Peter." She casts a light blanket out over the surface of his sleep.

"Our dinner's ready," says Richard.

He has broiled chicken and steamed asparagus and made a salad from the garden lettuce thinnings. They carry their plates and glasses of tea to the terrace. Their table is an empty construction wire spool; the mildewed canvas chairs they found in the spring time, behind a stack of rusting window screens.

Claire sits down cautiously and balances her plate on her knees. "It would be nice to have some decent lawn chairs," she says.

"That's what I like to hear," says Richard, "some good healthy materialism. And after the lawn chairs, then what? Come on, come on. A sofa? A kitchen sink?"

"Richard, you're making fun."

"That is not my intention. I consider myself a man of good will." He sets upon his food with gusto, he brandishes his fork. "It is one of my better qualities. Besides, I'm a family man now, I've got to think about these things."

She laughs outright, she is released into laughter.

"What did I say?" he asks with surprise. How young he looks!

"Well?" he repeats, for she has set down her plate and is leaning back in the chair, holding her abdomen.

Tears are in her eyes. "I don't know, I don't know." She tips back her head and draws in a deep breath. Above them the tree tops are dark against an opening of late blue through which with its short cry a nighthawk dives.

"Just wait," says Richard serenely, returning to his food. "You laugh, but just you wait." He slaps his chest, he straightens up. "You ain't seen nothing yet, baby."

High up a wind is gathering. Around the blue opening dark, feathery tree masses move as if under water. Tears come easily to her these days. Laughing or crying, it is all the same. After the winter will come another brief summer like this one, with the new child learning to walk, with strawberries, with peaches, with apples.

"Eat up before your food gets cold," says Richard.

High overhead the pure circle of blue, an unspent coin, deepens and deepens. How might it be possible, she asks herself, to grow into this value of blue?

She takes up her plate again.

"It's a good thing weekends are at least two days long," says Richard. "One day to get the kinks out and the next one to get down to business. Now, tomorrow: what about it?"

"I know what you're saying," she says.

"Well?"

All right, she says to herself. "All right," she says.

"You mean it? Steaming? Scraping? The whole bit?"

"Yes, I'm with you."

"Of course," she adds lightly, wickedly, "you do remember that it's the Lord's day, don't you?"

They stay on the terrace until the mosquitoes drive them in.

"Let's leave these dishes," says Richard as he comes up behind Claire at the sink. "Leave everything." Does her hair have the fragrance of strawberries, or is he just imagining?

Claire yawns and turns off the water.

"Come take a shower with me," says Richard.

She is very sleepy. She lets him wash her down. She accepts his helping hand as she steps out over the edge of the tub. He rubs himself dry and flings away the towel. "There!" he says, standing at attention in front of her. "I'm clean enough to eat off of." He grins significantly.

"Richard, you're indomitable."

"Yes," he says happily. He steers her down the hallway, he brings her to a halt in front of the south bedroom, he flicks on a bare overhead bulb. The wallpaper scrapings have been swept up and bagged. The battered steamer lies derelict in the center of the room.

"Look," says Claire, "a dead machine." She looks around; one wall is finished. "That's very nice, Richard. You really did a lot."

"Step in, step in," urges Richard.

She takes a few steps into the unfilled space.

"Where should the crib go, do you think?" asks Richard.

"Here," she says, "on this inside wall, at least in the wintertime." She puts her hands on her hips and turns all the way around. "The dresser there, I think, and the diaper table over here. I'm glad this is a sunny room. I'm glad—Richard! all we have is a mattress for your parents to sleep on."

"That's all right," says Richard quickly, shepherding her out of the room. "The floor will be good for my father's back."

They turn on no more lights. A breeze passes with them down the hallway. Claire stretches a hand out in front of her. Their own mattress on the floor is like a white island in the dark, or a boat riding on silver and dark water. The space around them seems to expand as they settle into each other. Walls fall away. She can close her eyes and be within a starry sky, seeing far down below a white patch, like an island, or a boat, or a continent.

Each day is an achievement, thinks Richard. To go successfully from beginning to end, to feel completed by action, that is an achievement. Success is golden, a fund of energy for the following day. Doesn't she think so? He will ask her when they are done kissing, he will find out if she, too, does not feel this tremendous, surging connection between one day and the next.

But by the time he is ready to speak to her, she is asleep, just like that. How close and shadowy she is! He listens to her breathing and for a moment, only a moment, feels bereft: off she has gone, without him, even in sleep accomplishing profundities.

Then he listens to the house, his house. He sighs contentedly. He lays an arm around Claire, which is easy to do, nested as they are in proximity to each other.

The Face of the Deep

Alan has told me that he was an orphan, but that is not strictly true. Living in this very city about a mile and a half up Lake Michigan is his grandmother, Lucie Annie, whom I am to meet for the first time tomorrow.

"Then you weren't really an orphan," I said tonight as I cleared up the dinner and Alan held forth from the center of the room. My kitchen is small, and I wove around his substantial body each time I crossed between table and sink.

"As good as," he said. "Lucie Annie went over the edge when my mother died and had to be put in the hospital. So for me there was no one left but Aunt Cassie."

"I see." I handed him a dish towel, which he accepted absently and then hung over his shoulder. I have never been embraced by Alan, but what I had been wanting to do all evening was put my arms around him, and not just because he considers himself an orphan. I continued rinsing dishes, however, resolved this time to be careful of myself.

"Lucie Annie did manage to pull herself together after a few years, but by then I was set up with Aunt Cassie."

"Did you come to visit your grandmother very often?"

"Hardly at all, hardly at all," said Alan as he began to pace the floor. "There was some nonsense between Cassie and her mother. Cassie stayed away, so I was kept away by circumstances. I've seen her more since I moved back here than I did in all those years combined." He stopped at the table and cut himself another large square of gingerbread. "Lucie Annie is—well, she's a rare bird, you'll see tomorrow. She'll like you. You take the time to listen."

Alan swallowed and smiled at me. His ancestors, he has told me, are Cornish, Swedish, German and Irish, blended in Wisconsin. His face is broad, his hair is fair and usually tousled, his grey eyes beneath straight brows are troubled and intelligent. His shirt is often carelessly tucked into his trousers. One morning when I met him in the vestibule by the mailboxes he had a residue of toothpaste on the corners of his mouth.

The first time he smiled directly at me I felt as if I had instantly been placed in relation to him, had in the gap of a second awakened to a new context. That was six weeks ago, the Saturday Angela and I were struggling up the stairs with my new thrift store reading chair. Alan opened the door on his landing and said, "Say there!" and without ado took the chair from us, practically ran with it up the next flight of stairs where he set it down, sat in it, and, laughing, said, "See what I did?" and then shot his smile directly down into my face and heart.

"If you are quite sure you are done eating, then we can go sit for a few minutes." My tone was bantering, as it might have been at work with the other librarians, but underneath all my words with him I struggle to find my bearings. Here I am again in the sway of charisma, and again it is confusingly mixed with disorder: Alan has been given a class of superior eighth grade students, and yet a year ago his wife left him, taking his son.

"Actually, I could use a glass of milk. That gingerbread is really good."

"Thank you," I said, and I felt that by providing me with the opportunity to pour white milk into a clear glass, which I could then hold out through air towards him, he was giving me a gift.

I led the way down the length of the apartment, which has the same floor plan as his directly below, to the small sun room at the east end. From my third floor windows I am allowed a slice of lake, above trees, between buildings; his view has slightly more city, slightly less lake.

It was dusky on the porch, but I kept the lights off so we could see what color was left in lake and sky. I was plucking a few yellowing leaves from my geraniums when Alan said, "I didn't tell you the whole truth about my father."

"In what way?" I sat down with my hands in my lap, holding the crushed leaves.

What he told me was not pleasant: an early disappearance, a tardy reappearance, alcoholism, fanatical views, a sordid death; but at that moment Alan's face in the dimness, the fragrance of geranium leaves, my own life expanded by him seemed more important than the vagaries of biography. I simply sat still, listening to a dark story until it was time for it to be over. Even now, with the force of his presence gone, I am thinking mainly about our outing tomorrow. If this fine September weather continues, we will take Lucie Annie for a picnic on the beach. She almost never gets out, Alan says. She is an old, frail woman.

I have taken a long bath. I have laid out blue jeans, a heavy sweater, a windbreaker, a blanket. To my parents I have written my weekly letter, again reassuring them that my move to the city, my new position, my apartment are providing me with even more than I had hoped. I turn out the light and in the dark am exquisitely aware of Alan's life below, as if joists and flooring were dissolving into a membrane within a single body. Again, without my knowing how it happens, my mind is filled with another person. I lie still, breathing with the world.

"What you will find about Lucie Annie," says Alan in the car, preparing me, "is that she can make good sense one minute and be spaced out the next. That doesn't stop her from talking all the time, though."

"How can she possibly do that when you're around?"

"She and I make a pair, all right." Alan laughs and turns his face, just for a moment as if he is really seeing me, but long enough for me to have been given a glimpse of myself against a backdrop of water.

The views we are having along the lake drive promise a feast day of blues shimmered with white.

"There's the boat that dredges up lead from the shooting range," says Alan.

"Yes, I see it sometimes from the bus on my way to work. Who uses the range anyway?"

"Sportsmen. Reservists. I'm not sure," says Alan.

"Have you ever been in the military?"

"No, I've always been exempt for one reason or another."

Now for me it is as if his wife has come to sit in the car between us. Over the weeks Alan has not defined why we are becoming friends, and I do not know myself. We met on the stairs, at the mailbox, at the fish market; we cooked salmon steaks together; two weeks ago he came up the back fire escape to talk to me while I sanded a chest of drawers; last Sunday we walked to the art museum and back; to-day, another Sunday, is Lucie Annie day. Towards this unknown wife, older than myself, I have on occasion felt self-righteous: if I had been she, I tell myself, I would not have been inconstant; I would have stayed and gone deeper. Now, riding beside the cold lake, I feel my cheeks flush as I imagine a tenderness that has not been asked of me.

Alan turns away from the lake onto a shaded street. One early maple is already a bouquet of red. The houses quickly change from grandiose to modest, and after several blocks Alan pulls to the curb in front of a stucco bungalow. He lays his arm behind my head and peers out my window to the drawn blinds.

"There it is," he says, "the home place. It's a good thing the heating season hasn't started yet."

"Why is that?" I ask. Alan's profile is close to me now, the blond brows, the grey irises of his eyes, the near cheek with a patch of stubble missed by the razor. He had still been buttoning his shirt and pulling on his sweater this morning when he ran up the stairs to knock on my door.

"Well, it's this way." He turns amused, testing eyes on me. "Lucie Annie doesn't like to be away from her furnace because she's afraid it might blow up."

"Goodness, I never think about furnaces."

"No?" he says, smiling, still watching me, still testing.

I walk towards the house harboring his look. For a moment, as we wait for the door to be opened, he places his hand on the small of my back, a small gesture that touches my blood. "Thanks for coming along today," he says.

I hear the turning of several locks and a dull clacking that turns out to be jar lids, punctured, strung like buttons and hung from the inner door handle.

Lucie Annie holds a housecoat to her throat with a thin hand. "Oh my dears, I am so terribly, terribly slow today, you must forgive me. I thought I would be quite ready for you, but here I am, as you see. You're going to think I'm senile." She takes Alan's arm and leans against him, all the while brightly smiling at me. Does she eat? I am wondering. Soda crackers, perhaps; tea.

"This is Bridget Davies," says Alan.

"My dear," says Lucie Annie, reaching out her hand. "You are so sweet to come, and I had planned to be entirely ready for you, but as you can see, I am just another fragment of the ruinous disorder in this house." She waves an arm gaily in the direction of a dim living room that appears to be littered with books and papers. The chairs and couch are covered with blankets. The venetian blinds are drawn. Slightly thrown off balance, she clings again to Alan's arm and looks up at him. "Oh, I have made no progress at all, none at all. I'm just as naughty as I was—no, worse. All I seem to do is move things from one place to another. And now here you are with this lovely friend." She reaches out towards me again, and I take her hand. "My dear, you are sweet to come, and you both look splendid, such lovely warm sweaters." She is holding on tightly to both of us, kneading our arms. "You must watch your step. Alan knows all about my towers of empty cans. Do you think I am silly? Well, you may say what you like, I think it is one of the cleverest and least expensive alarm systems yet devised. The only trouble is that I knock them over myself." She laughs at herself with apparent delight.

I look down to my feet, and there indeed are three tin cans, labels removed, stacked end to end as in a child's game. I step around them as Lucie Annie draws us into the living room.

"Please do not mind my voice, I do not have a cold," she says to me. "My cords have changed, that's why I sound like an old creaking door. And to think that years ago I had elocution lessons. Did you know that, Alan? All those lessons, and I still sound like an old door!'' She shakes between us with a laughter that Alan and I quickly join. "That was the year I was kept out of school for my weak constitution. Reverend Jarvis, you see, was given Sunday dinner by my mother. And I wasn't getting a bit stronger until he suggested that she discontinue those medicines.''

"Lucie Annie, you're going to need some warm clothes today,'' says Alan rather loudly. "It's a nice day, but it's going to be cooler at the lake.''

By degrees he induces her to go upstairs and dress. "Open a few of those blinds, Alan.'' She turns to waver a finger at him from the first landing. "I am preserving the carpet, but I'm sure you young people will want more light.''

After pacing a few moments in front of the windows, running his hands through his hair, looking at me and then away, Alan decides to leave now to pick up some sandwiches.

"I should have brought the rest of the gingerbread,'' I say.

"No, no. Today is my treat.'' He slaps his wallet pocket, and as the door slams, setting off a clacking of jar lids, I have a thought that I might be left here with Lucie Annie all day.

From the depths of one of the blanket-draped chairs I survey the room: open and glass-covered bookshelves, chairs and small tables set at odd angles, piles of papers, clippings, letters, books everywhere, even on the floor. The light is brownish, like sediment.

I have gotten up and am examining an old painting, oil on wood, framed in walnut, when Lucie Annie comes back down. She is wearing a tweed suit, inside which she seems to have shrunk, and canvas shoes.

"I feel that I have forgotten something essential,'' she says.

I tell her, unsure exactly how to pitch my voice, that Alan has gone out for sandwiches.

"He is a dear, helpful boy. He has charm, I think that would be the correct word. And I see you have gone straight to one of my prizes.'' She indicates the painting—a primitively executed domestic interior, men, women, children clustered about fireplace and table. There are clay pipes, yarn in a basket, stiff children like miniature adults. The women look wizened. The heads of the men are bent sharply forward, almost like angle irons, from the base of the neck. Still, it must be a festive occasion: there are bits of lace in bodices, dark suits.

"Those are the Cornish miners in Wisconsin," says Lucie Annie. "Cassie wanted it, but I wouldn't let it go because I don't trust that husband of hers." She begins a sigh, from which she shakes herself free. "The marriages in our family have all been very difficult, I am afraid."

I lean closer to the faded, stunted figures. I am about to ask her if the mining tunnels were really so low as to have caused that much distortion when she says, "I was telling you about Reverend Jarvis, wasn't I? Now he was the one with a voice like an angel. If you could have heard him, you would have said the same. A heavenly voice. He could hold us in the palm of his hand."

During the half hour trip to the state park beach, I sit in the back of the car, at first leaning forward against the front seat so as to join in the conversation, but then, tiring, sinking back into a corner. To my right is a mile of high fertile flat land that ends abruptly in sky. The lake is only intermittently visible, but I am glad to know it is there. The farms in the distance look prosperous, simplified, freshened.

Alan is still telling Lucie Annie about his special class. "To think of that, to think of that," she has said a number of times.

"At that age," says Alan, "they can learn anything."

Now and then in the midst of his talk he glances back to wink charmingly at me. What he gives his students, he has told me, is himself, dramatized—he can't help being an actor; but more than that he tries simply to open doors and then not stand in the way. With his wife, about whom he has only spoken to me once, he said he also tried to be unobstructing, but precisely on this point apparently failed.

His wife had had a dream, he told me last Sunday on our walk to the museum, in which he had been a giant barring the exit to a house. She had slipped between his legs and run away down the hill to a town by the ocean. Shortly after that she had in reality left him and returned to Connecticut, back with their son to her parents' house, back to school. Regression, he said to me, shaking his head in half-hearted pronouncement, but his voice in telling the story had been flat, like a hand opened out.

He has not asked me much about myself, and I have not told him. What he sees, I believe, is someone who goes competently forth each day and comes back cheerfully enough at night; he does not know how grateful I am to be able to do that much.

The road to the park winds through sand dunes down to water level. The light has stayed clear. It is eleven o'clock. Lucie Annie ties a grey net bonnet under her chin. She has brought along a navy blue raincoat and a worn handbag. Her smile, as she allows me to help her out of the car, is almost girlish. There is an off-shore wind across the nearly deserted parking lot, and Lucie Annie quickly takes my arm. "The first time I ever saw this lake was when I was being courted," she says. "Oh, Helmut was ever so attentive in those days. Such nice little trips he planned."

"What was your husband's work?" I ask.

"Engineering, electrical engineering. Now there was a precise man. One day when I was upset I backed the car down the driveway and straight into a tree, and then, oh, didn't he chastise me dreadfully and didn't I chastise myself, but do you know what the doctor said to me later, that dear, helpful man who pulled me through? He said, Lucie Annie you plainly had a good deal to be upset *about*. Now those were some of the kindest words I ever had spoken to me."

Alan has slammed shut the trunk of the car and is motioning us forward. He carries a brown paper sack and an armload of blankets. The lake ahead is a soothing band of blue.

"Because you see," continues Lucie Annie, standing still, "up until then it had always been my nerves that had been blamed for everything. My mother had no nerves; I was supposedly the one with the nerves. But do you want to know something? The very month that my mother died—I was fifty years old, mind you—was when I finally got over my fear of being alone in the dark. Now explain that to me." She sounds triumphant.

"What are you saying, Lucie Annie?" Alan has shifted his load and come to take her other arm. Together, the wind at our backs, we approach the white sand.

"I am presenting this sweet friend of yours with a conundrum."

Alan looks at me over Lucie Annie's head. "And what answers does my friend have?"

"She is contemplating," I say, returning his gaze.

"One of the benefits of growing older," says Lucie Annie between us, "is that you can finally speak your mind."

"You'll notice, Lucie Annie," says Alan jovially, "that I have lost no time in assuming that prerogative for myself."

Lucie Annie leans her head for a moment against his shoulder. "And well you should have, dear boy, for what else were you left with besides your wits and your own voice? It's very old-fashioned, I think, not to let children speak out for themselves."

Carried along by the wind and our linked bodies, I am silent, contemplating our common mysteries, of which Lucie Annie is today's example.

We are at the edge of the water now, on firmer sand. Lucie Annie bends with difficulty to select a wet grey pebble, marbled with green. She straightens up and ecstatically faces out to open water.

"Such a view!" she exclaims. "Such a glorious view!" Steadying herself between us, she takes a series of great, deep breaths.

Very quickly afterwards, however, she begins noticeably to tire. We have gone only a short way up the beach when she begins muttering something to herself; her eyes are downcast.

"This way, Lucie Annie," says Alan. "We'll find a place out of the wind. I had some tea put in a thermos for you."

We turn from the lake and slowly work our way up between the dunes, skirting patches of coarse grass and creeping juniper, searching for a sheltered pocket. A few cottonwoods and aspen tremble in the midday light just beyond the first ridge of dunes; then beyond us there is a broad, swooping basin of sand and low growth before the shadowed forest begins.

"Just a bit more, Lucie Annie," says Alan.

Her head is down; she seems almost to hang between us. Rounding a tufted mound of sand, we come abruptly upon a pair of lovers, oblivious, deeply connected. Alan veers; I veer; Lucie Annie might be asleep except that her feet are moving forward. My eyes are smarting.

When at last we settle her upon a blanket, her eyes are closed. She leans back against an incline of sand, and Alan draws a second blanket over her. She murmurs something, he bends close to catch it, nods, and pats her shoulder.

I am sitting a little off to one side, blowing my nose. Then I get up and walk away. I bound down into the swooping basin of sand, heels first. When I feel out of sight, I let myself slide down upon the sand and turn my tears to the sky. There is nothing overhead, not a cloud, not a hawk nor a crow, nothing but a lucid September blue under which I wish I could abandon all these old griefs.

Alan comes up beside me and crouches down and takes my hand. I roll onto my side so that I can look at him, crouching against a sweeping background of sand. His son, he has told me, is his spitting image, as if he had given birth to him himself, straight out of his mouth.

I have no child. It is my own ignorant youth that weighs on me.

"Is Lucie Annie all right?" I ask.

He nods, reaching out to touch my wet cheek. "She just needs these little naps." He lifts my hair bit by bit away from my cheek. My breath catches, I sigh, and then little by little, as I suppose I have to, I tell him my story, the part that has been opened again by the lovers: an ordinary story, probably, of enthrallment and disillusion, to which I nevertheless still in puzzlement cling.

He strokes my hand. "So," he says, "and where is this fellow now?"

"In the mountains, with a group. I think our time together was no more than the blink of an eye to him, a quick step."

"And you wanted continuance, I suppose."

"Well, yes, I thought I did."

"Ah, yes, of course." He flings himself back on the sand, as if flung back into his own ache. Both of us now are facing the sky, still holding hands. My breath quietens. This draw of sand, beneath the main currents of the wind, is like a cradle.

When we return to Lucie Annie, her eyes are open, but she has stayed beneath the blanket. She looks as if she wants to be praised for having had a nap.

"You're bright-eyed and bushy-tailed, Lucie Annie," says Alan.

"My dears, I am simply basking in this day. When I was a child I dreamed of getting to the shore, you see. It was always a dream."

She sits up to accept the plastic cup of tea from Alan. Net bonnet askew, raincoat bunched about her shoulders, the freshness of rest on her cheeks, she gazes out upon the lake, where I see now a purplish cast near the horizon and across the waves areas of green, like floating beds of emeralds.

"I have never known my Bible as well as I should," says Lucie Annie, "but a great piece of water like this always recalls to me the face of the deep."

She reaches out to grip my arm and asks, "Are you religious, my dear?"

I sense Alan's eyes on me, but my own eyes want to stay upon the water. Above it, I think, is the ancient, dividing firmament and beyond that lights and darknesses and waters unfathomable.

"I believe in growth," I finally hear myself saying, with relief, to Lucie Annie.

On Monday morning's bus I sway in company with other passengers. Where I look, I see life: a blue doorway in an alley, the Chinaman sweeping the walk in front of his bookstore, a girl with her hand to her hair. The lake under a slightly overcast sky is a tender, milky blue. As the bus lurches to a stop across from the library, I step lightly down, pass the seedy bridal shop on the corner where pinched-in mannequins encased in awkward folds of material gesture blindly upwards, step lightly into the street, step along to work on my own feet.

Overhead pigeons wheel among inner city buildings. A favorite roosting place is an upper-story ledge of the library, above a long row of stone wreaths, though many of the birds land upon the broad entry steps or within the Corinthian portico, in company at almost any hour of the day with at least two or three homeless street people. Today Ellen, one of those I know by name, is seated at the base of a column in a patch of weak sunlight, her shopping bags arranged around her. She wears a hat onto which she has affixed fluttering scraps of cloth and paper.

"Good morning, Ellen," I say.

Walleyed, she seems to take me in, but her voice is an undirected incantation. "No seafood to see, no sirloin to chop. Nothing. Nothing. Nothing."

"No breakfast, Ellen?" I take out two quarters and crouch down to open her hand and close her fingers around the coins. Then quickly I am up, passing through the huge doors and across the mosaic floor of the entry hall, past the potted palms and blond marble columns. Two coins are dropped into the sea, swallowed, and does the sea change?

All I know today is that I am in this selfsame sea. Last night I dreamt that my body dangled in great depths, my arms stretched out upon the surface of the water; I was kept afloat by my attentive breaths just above the rocking waves.

Angela smiles at me from her station behind the reference telephone, the receiver already saddled upside down on her shoulder, a book open in front of her. My place is at the humanities desk, just outside the doors of the main reading room.

All morning the street people in their many layers of dun cloth make their way past our desk towards resting places. A stout, off-duty watchman in green with bulbous nose and closely shaved neck, keys still clipped to his waist, selects a Polish magazine. Two Vietnamese girls with exquisite faces bend over a school project. Several shabby gentlemen, regulars to the room, look down their noses upon morning papers. Ellen sleeps, her head to her chest, beside a globe in a wooden stand. Dozens of people, hundreds of people breathe within these capacious rooms. My duties take me here and there. I am swimming usefully in life.

"Come in," Alan said to me yesterday afternoon on our return from the beach. He seemed quieter than usual. He made a pot of tea and carried it to his sunporch.

I asked if I should run up for the gingerbread.

"All right," he said. He had one arm thrown over his head against the back of the canvas sling chair, and he was looking out the window.

Many of Alan's belongings must be vestiges of married life, but his rooms have the quality of not being thoroughly lived in.

I came back with the gingerbread and handed him a generous piece on a napkin. He ate with absorption, every now and then looking at his watch. Sunday nights he calls his son; sometimes he is allowed to speak to him, sometimes not.

We talked a bit about Lucie Annie, her state of health, her situation. Had he ever considered boarding with her? I asked.

"Oh my God," he said, "does it seem to you that I should?"

I told him I was just asking.

After a little while I took my leave. I went up to my own rooms and had a bath and scrambled an egg and got into bed with a book of stories. I thought the telephone might ring, but when it did not, I became comfortable with the silence.

I must have slept extraordinarily well last night because all today I have had the energetic sensation of being slightly taller than myself.

"You're in a hurry," says Angela in the ladies' room at five o'clock. I am pinning back my hair. I take a quick survey of myself, pinch my cheeks and then meet Angela's calm, broad face in the mirror. When she was a child, she trekked with her aunt out of Nazi Germany; twice the aunt was raped; Angela even remembers the smells along the road.

"I guess I am," I say.

Am I expecting something? Out on the portico I pause to take in the mellow, moted sunlight, slanting in now beneath the clouds.

Surprise! he would say if he were waiting for me behind a column. It would be his style: a dramatic meeting, a bit of swaggering, a hand upon my back.

And we would go down some steps to a restaurant, and he would say, All day I have been, and I would say, All day I have been.

Down the steps of the library I go alone, stepping around birds, stepping ahead as the light changes. I am surprised how quickly the bus comes, how quickly the scene changes to one of going home.

The lake has taken on more color. At the shooting range targets in crude human shape, painted black, have been set up along the water's edge. To me inside the bus the shots sound as if they are thudding inside boxes.

At the corner market I buy an Idaho potato, a carton of cottage cheese and a bunch of broccoli. All along the side street the sunlight rushes in.

My mailbox is stuffed with a magazine, which I look through briefly, leaning against the newel post.

Then up I go, step by step. An empty stairwell. Nearing the second landing, I am surprised to see Alan's door ajar. My eyes rise to the level of his carpet, his easy chair, his briefcase and jacket, his coffee table; to his blue couch against the far wall. There I see him asleep, of human size, mouth relaxed, hands upon his chest, knees slightly bent and splayed. I see his brown socks, his wristwatch, his thick, interlaced fingers, his neck below his ear, his shadowed, lidded eye.

Quietly I reach out and pull the door closed. Perhaps, hearing a click, he dreams that the door has come open upon his sleep. He will wake and find himself safe.

For a moment in the dimmed stairwell I stand still, biting upon the knuckles of my hand. Far away in Connecticut I see his wife cutting into a loaf of bread, feeding his son. This boy turns from Granny's window and wants to know if the boats he sees can go all the way from Connecticut to Wisconsin, all the way on the same water.

What is there to say?

I climb the rest of the stairs, scrub my potato and set it to bake. I rinse and slit two stalks of the broccoli. I pour a glass of apple juice and take it to the fire escape off the kitchen where a short while of sunlight remains upon the bricks, upon the locust tree beside the alley below, upon my own limbs.

I drink from my glass. Is something essential lacking? I take a deep, preparatory breath.

Parts of Speech

It is said that bicycle riding, like swimming, like walking itself, once learned is never a lost ability, as if, Julia Trilling is to think in her triumph, there were a conduit between mind and body labelled Balance Upon Two Wheels, which once reamed out and upheld by sufficient health, remains clear forever. In motion through the open air she is to become like water to herself, pouring from one place into another with a simplicity she had nearly forgotten.

The bicycle was her brother's suggestion. At the age of fifty-seven? Julia at first laughed. She would fall, she said; she would get rattled in traffic.

But Christopher Scott liked solutions, especially his own. A bicycle would give her a new focus after her vigil with Milton, new perspectives, soothing exercise; it was exactly the thing. Then, the idea planted, he said no more. Thirty years of real estate development had taught him a great deal about timing. He also knew Julia, in her own way a genius at picking up every scrap that chanced into her ken, finding its advantage, making large things come about: children, friendships, work, houses, gardens, golden occasions. Even in Milton Trilling's dying she had seemed to Christopher sublime in her ability to fling together from those unfavorable, fragmented months an almost exalted sense of living. But now had come the time, he reasoned, for her to shift into a new phase, and in his practical way he was trying to help.

In April, in the presence of all four of Julia's nearly-grown children, home after the funeral, he said to her *bicycle* and then waited.

She protested that she would be too stiff to peer around properly, but Sally said, "Nonsense, Mother, I'll give you exercises. Get down on the floor."

Stretched out on the living room carpet, looking up into Sally's smooth face, tanned from a winter in the mountains, Julia followed instructions to move arms, legs, head, spine. "Think of each vertebra, Mother. Think of stretching everything very gently."

"So," Julia paused, "the egg shall teach the hen, is that it?"

"This isn't something brand new, Mother."

Julia submitted to her child, glad enough at the moment to have someone else directing her. To do this and then that, to feel one way and then another: what was the purpose of those passionate rhythms? She had done all she had known how to do and still Milton had died.

Sally taught her how to turn her head one way and bend her knee over her body the other way and so very gently twist, twist. Her spine made cracking noises like a piece of dry furniture.

"Mine does the same thing," Sally reassured her. "You should get down here, too, Uncle Christopher."

Avuncular, on the domestic sidelines, come from his bachelor rooms to take another measured draught of family life, he found himself complying, for the sake of the bicycle. Death is a closing and an opening, he thought as he hitched up his neat trousers and eased himself down near Julia. There was a euphoria in the household, hilarity irrepressibly ballooning out through grief, the joys of reunion being stronger after all. He was almost grateful to old Milt for his part in this high drama.

"Your hamstrings are tight, Uncle Christopher. Lift your leg in the air and turn your toes toward your chest. Doesn't that feel good?"

Christopher wasn't sure, but a moment of largeness seemed to overtake him. He looked across a well-worn patch of carpet to Julia, who so closely resembled him in whiteness, in pinkness, in girth, and winked.

He thinks me remarkable, she thought, weariness and loss pulling at her like undertow; even at this drastic time he looks to me for the generation of life; he humors me; he cares for his own comfort. Then, ashamed of herself—for how droll and capable he always was, how glad she always was to see him—she closed her eyes. The voices of her children rose and fell, vital, beautiful voices; the children, at any rate, never mind about herself and Christopher, were indeed remarkable. Now they were fatherless. She opened her eyes and swept up all her grown babies in a glance. Would they be all right? Was she strong enough to hold them, each one, safe within her bereft mind alone?

Then it came time, as it had to, for ordinary days to recommence. Paul, the eldest of the children, returned to his job at the art museum, Sally, the geologist, to the mountains, Martha to architecture school, John, the most difficult of the four, to college. Christopher was in and out of town, absorbed in assembling, with one eye on historic preservation and the other on economics, a substantial package for a downtown block in the state capital.

Julia returned to her fifth-grade class, to those inquisitive, messy, exuberant ten-year-olds she had taught for the last fifteen years. "Nouns name things," she said on her first day back, an exceptionally warm day for late April. "And verbs tell what happens to things." She was teaching with her back to the open windows because that was the direction upon which the children's attention seemed fixed anyway. Now and then she herself turned to look out into second-story sky. She remembered clearly being ten years old: she remembered being happy, happy going to bed at night, in the morning waking happy. That was the year she had first been conscious of loving a boy. Together after school each day she and he had dug into the side of a hill in a vacant lot to make a house of earth.

"What is perhaps hardest of all," she ventured one evening to Christopher, who had brought in a dinner for them both, "is that Milton really isn't *here.*" Could anything, she wondered, have prepared her for the physicality of his nonappearance? It was not that she kept expecting him to turn up here or there, she said, gesturing, in his reading chair or in the bathtub, but rather that she knew with palpable precision that he would not.

Then she fell silent. She carried a burden of unspoken words. There were simple things she wanted to know, which she did not think she could find out from Christopher, which even she and Milton had not known how to milk from speech in all those months of illness. She wanted to know about love, their love: what was it in the face of death? She wanted to know about herself: who was she now in the face of what she had not been able to do, to say? Her courage had not taken the form of such questions of the heart; his had not been able to convey to her the inner shapes of that which was overtaking him.

After the first shock of his illness had been absorbed, they had both seemed to perpetrate, with an almost impregnable fortitude, a daily life nearly as crowded as it always had been with the fluctuating realities of work, children, friends, concern for the world. Everyone had seemed to find them magnificent. They had done everything they had known how to do. Yet now in the wake of their active life together, Julia was left with a muteness as perceptible as the absence of Milton himself.

One warm night in May, sleepless, she paced the upstairs hallway of the house, past doorways where in another age of keeping watch she had once listened for the breathing of children. A scent of lilac reached her. In a moment, a raincoat over her nightgown, she was in the backyard, facing the fragrant, massy lilacs, which were color-drained, almost black—she looked and looked more deeply—not really black, no, but a combination of darknesses, what she knew to be daytime purple and green now greyed into another order of swaying color.

The melanoma had spread to Milton Trilling's brain, into the mind that had been his livelihood. They had not known in the gradual decline of one day into the next what functions might become impaired. Colors had become confused: red and green: he had described this to her as he handed over his car keys. And yet up until his last month, incoherent on some other matters, he could still deliver almost flawlessly an old lecture in intellectual history.

In the night yard Julia lay down flat on the picnic table near the lilacs and looked skywards, a single moist pyramid of plucked blossom held upon her chest. She had five senses. She was still alive, still in this world. It would still happen that she would do one thing, then another; feel this way and then that. With an open face she sent her questions upwards. The clear sky offered down layer upon spangled layer of itself.

That night, tenderly, weeping freely, she lifted armloads of Milton's clothes from their bedroom closet. She laid his sweaters and scarves and gloves and pajamas into boxes. She stood for a long time above the shallow top bureau drawer, contemplating wooden trays of keys and tie pins and coins. Finally she carried everything down the hall to Paul's room, a temporary disposition like those she had been making all her married life—goods moved inconclusively from one place to another.

It was really astonishing how crowded with objects this large, shabby, serviceable house appeared now, how much domestic disorder she and Milton had managed to overlook. It was upon the children and their own work they had concentrated. Julia paused in bedroom doorways; she opened the linen closet in the hallway; she sat on the top step of the stairwell and looked down into a gloaming of furniture. How attached was she to all of this? It might be easy enough, she thought, to turn the whole operation over to her children and simply walk away. They should take it, she would say, take the hot water bottles and pillows and toasters and encyclopedias and Christmas tree stands and make it all happen again. It would be their turn. And she? She would pose her questions in a new context.

Julia! She could almost hear what Christopher's response would be. Your children aren't ready yet. Think of the holidays, the celebrations! Think of us all! Think of me! Christopher. One Christmas years ago when the children were small he had given her a large brownish shawl, had draped it himself around her and called her Mother Earth: absurdly rhapsodic he could be sometimes, and fastidious, and opinionative; innocent, too, of the real labors of family life.

The next Saturday she rolled up her thick white hair as usual, tied a scarf over her head, fetched a push broom from the basement and went out to the garage. She intended nothing more radical today than a bit of sweeping so that she could organize the gardening tools and get on out to the flower beds. Usually by this time in the spring she would have raked clear all the perennials and made the ground ready for the annuals. With the broad garage doors open to the sunlight, she swept at old leaves and debris, moved equipment, swept again, and so it was that she put her hands upon the black, substantial, three-speed English bicycle, abandoned years ago by the girls for slender, racy French ten-speeds. The fenders of the English model had even been removed in an early yearning towards the ideal of swiftness and lightness; these rusty arcs now were slung over the bare rear tire, which was flat, of course. Julia lifted them off and wheeled the bicycle into the central space. She stepped into the frame. She squeezed the hand brakes and flipped the gear lever, which seemed a little tight between second and third, but at least the cables were connected. One foot rocking a pedal back and forth, she looked up from the machine and out to the bright sloping driveway. Christopher was right, anyway, about her needing exercise. Tending illness, aching for someone else, had a way of making you forget what plain health could be.

So it was that Julia progressed during the last week in May, from that Saturday of walking the bicycle to the Varsity Cycle Shop and half-walking it, half-riding it home along sidewalks, to a steadiness that took her first into her own quiet street and then into the traffic of other neighborhoods. Every day after school she changed into an old cotton skirt, tied a scarf around her head and took a long turn before dinner.

Careful, her slightly smiling face open to the breeze, she transformed, by the steady motion of her legs, houses and gardens and shops into a variegated trail behind her. She felt on the forefront of herself, like water just tilting over the edge of a vessel. If the going got rough, she dismounted and walked. Every night before bed she lay down on a certain place on the bedroom carpet beneath the double windows and put herself through a program of gentle exercises. Thursday it rained, and, kept inside her cluttered house, she thought about the bicycle.

On his return to town that Saturday, Christopher was surprised to find Julia not at home at five o'clock. He had come cheerily up the tulip-lined driveway, poking now and then with his umbrella tip at the later perennials shoving their way up through the matted leaves of the still unraked border, and had expected to find Julia in the backyard or the screened porch or the kitchen. He had expected to hear the radio or the television. He had been expecting a drink and the opportunity to burst his buttons a little about securing that last parcel of land: the puzzle was now complete; the intricacies of financing were almost worked out; it was the largest project he had ever put his hands upon.

The house was unlocked. He went in through the kitchen, called her name downstairs and upstairs, helped himself to gin and tonic and settled himself in the living room to wait. He had worked nearly a hundred hours that week. The evening paper was thrown upon the front porch, but Christopher stayed immobile and pleased within the flush of his own well-earned news. Sparrows were gathering, twittering, in the ivy that covered the high windows on either side of the fireplace. Such a pleasant, well-used room it was, such a pleasant house! Up those stairs he sometimes had trod when one of the children was sick. Ho! Ho! What have we here? A nephew who says he's sick? Into that dining room with the cranberry walls he had often advanced with Milton for deeply satisfying meals set upon white cloths: turkeys, roasts, browned potatoes, garden tomatoes, winter squash; laughter, free speech, confirmation.

He tipped back his head and at that moment glimpsed Julia peddling up the driveway, one colorful second of Julia on a bicycle.

Well, he thought, well. . . . He sipped at his drink, priming himself for his glowing rendition of victory among the streets of business. And good for Julia; she really had done it, his sister.

"Christopher?" He heard her opening the refrigerator. "Why did you park down on the street?" she called.

"And miss the chance of nodding to all those tulips?" She came in on bare feet. "What's that you're drinking?" he asked. "It looks like milk."

"It is. Welcome back." She kissed him on the cheek, sank down in the chair opposite and raised her rather dirty feet to the coffee table.

"You haven't been cycling barefooted, I hope."

"How absurd!" she laughed. "Listen, I've been places today."

But how should she tell him? The idea was still the tenderest infant. "I decided to go out Willow Road past the dairy," she began. That much was easy, but now she wanted to protect what had come next: the undulating blacktop road out of town, the grassy ditches, the turn to the right, the turn to the left, the old limestone chapel with curtains in the window, a sign saying Honey For Sale and a graveyard full of shooting stars; then her prize, her newborn—a paintless, abandoned farmhouse, a windmill such as her children used to build with their erector sets, broken in half with its blades sunk in the deep grass, a dilapidated barn, lilacs gone wild, her own breath scarcely existing in her excitement as she dropped her bicycle and waded up to the porch where she saw through a dirty window a parlor emptied of everything; then her thirst, her search back to the chapel for water and information: who owned the house, and might it be for rent? No, this she could not tell Christopher, not yet; this she must leap over. "I went out several miles at least," she said, "and got tremendously thirsty and found the most wonderful tiny woman who lives in a church and who gave me coffee and bread with home-grown honey. Yes, she keeps bees. And do you know what she said? Christopher, listen to this: she said, 'You don't have to be crazy to keep bees, but it helps.' Isn't that marvelous?"

Julia laughed, more gaily than she had in months, took a drink of milk and looked at Christopher, who was dressed today in a dapper, pale grey suit. Was her house safe? Yes, of course; she had said nothing. A small image secretly, safely breathed, of herself plunged for a summer into grass, into wildflowers, into a spaciousness of empty rooms and weather and far-reaching views. So, she said to Christopher, and how was he? Enough now about her adventures.

Well, said Christopher, smiling, as a matter of fact he did have a little sweet news himself, but first he must congratulate her on the bicycle. She looked radiant. There was an extraordinary blueness to her eyes today. He hadn't expected her to go quite so far afield, so soon, but obviously the exercise was doing her good.

Yes, she said, he had been right: it was exactly the thing.

Later Christopher wanted to know if she had heard yet from Johnny about the summer. His offer of a job still stood.

Not a word, she said. That rascal. Was he spoiled, she implored, or had he had too much benign neglect? She was trying not to pester him, not to worry.

Christopher folded his hands over his chest. Well, he drawled out finally, he'd have to be the first to admit the value of going one's own way.

That night, as she was falling asleep, Julia listened to the wind and thought about her youngest son. She sighed and turned her face into the pillow. Johnny. She would try not to worry. She would put him in her mind—there, just like that, gently within the folds of her caring—and then think about something else: she would think about the little house, what minimum she would need to take with her if she were to rent it for a few months: a mattress, a pan or two, her books and watercolors, a lamp, the bicycle strapped to the car.

At last she slept, and she dreamed that Milton was lying beneath a white shroud, dead, but moving, heaving his shoulders, wanting to be helped alive. Quickly overcoming her fear, she rushed to him and lifted his head and held him against her breast. Was there anything she could get for him? she asked, stroking his hair. Yes, he said, a drink of water. Then he lifted his face to hers and said clearly, in his voice before illness, "I bring you good news of the brotherhood."

Immediately, soaked with a sweet sweat, she awoke. Calm moonlight shone upon the familiar mahogany dresser, the oak rocking chair. She changed her nightgown. How strange, she thought calmly, how strange.

The next day at noon, this time in her car, followed by a pickup truck driven by a slight, white-haired farmer named Kaiser, she turned for the second time up the rutted drive. It had been his wife's home place, Kaiser said as they walked to the porch, but after the folks had died they hadn't had the wherewithal to keep the buildings up. "No one wants buildings nowadays," he said, selecting a key on his ring. "They don't pay. Land don't even pay much." He pushed his shoulder against the door and then stepped aside for Julia to enter.

The floor was painted pine, a worn brown; the walls had been papered long ago in forget-me-nots; the plain woodwork was an alligatored, painted brown. Julia stepped into a kitchen where cracked, yellowing linoleum stretched unevenly to a back door. "May I open this?" she asked Kaiser, and he found another key on his ring and pulled open the dull kitchen door upon a juicy, sun-struck, singing density of lilac, grass, hedgerow, ploughed field, sky. It was as if a lid had just been taken off nature.

"How much would you rent the house for?" asked Julia. "Just for the summer."

"This house don't have the conveniences," said Kaiser, regarding her closely.

Julia crossed to the rust-stained sink and turned a faucet.

"Them pipes are all empty."

"But there would be water?"

Kaiser crossed his arms over his thin chest. "No water now except maybe in the rain cistern. The windmill went down a few years ago, and I took out the gas generator for my own place. The folks never converted. They didn't much like the electric company."

"But could you hook it up again?" asked Julia.

"It's a lot of work," said Kaiser. "I says to Minnie, 'What does she want to see that old place for?' and Minnie says, 'You go show her anyway because she's got this strong hankering.' "

"I see." Julia turned off the faucet of air. She thought of lucky Minnie in her one-room church, surrounded only by bees and flowers and gravestones. "What about the cistern?" asked Julia.

Kaiser pointed to a hand pump outside the back door. "You can't drink rainwater," he said.

Julia went outside anyway and stood on the pebbly cement by the pump. The air was bright and humming. The iron handle was warm. Scree-oke, scree-oke, she began to pump.

"It might've leaked dry," said Kaiser.

Julia felt a rush of stubbornness within herself, but the handle only moved up and down, up and down without resistance, like a sleeve without an arm. "Well," she said at last, lifting away her hand, now stained orange, "nothing comes." She turned away from the pump and from Kaiser in the doorway and looked out upon the overgrown barnyard, where buildings tended downwards to a vigorous, weedy bed of green. She pressed her lips together. Was she sane? she wondered.

Finally she turned. "Mr. Kaiser, you are probably right that the house is unsuitable, but I would like to ask a favor. May I stay here the rest of the afternoon? I would lock up and bring the key to you. I would just like to sit here for a little while.'' She opened her purse. ''Here.''

''Well,'' said Kaiser without moving, squinting out to the horizon. ''You can keep your money. I don't mind if you sit.'' He unhooked a key. ''This here is for the back door. Leave it off with Minnie. She's more on your way. I don't mind.''

He stopped just as he was turning the corner of the house towards the front door. ''That kitchen,'' he said, pointing, ''used to be a bedroom. My wife was born in it.'' He raised a hand to Julia, and as he turned away she noticed the stiffness of his gait, the slackness of his overalls, the emptiness of his hands; he was someone of her generation, she thought, whom she might never see again.

''Thank you!'' she called out.

She stood in place until she saw him cross from the front of the house to the truck. Then she raised her hand to him: *good luck.*

The truck jounced down the drive and onto the blacktop to the north; almost a mile down the road to the south, at the crossroads, stood Minnie's diminutive yellow stone church on the slight rise of land, a single tree in front, behind it a white outhouse the size of Julia's fingernail and a dotting of beehives, fields planted right up to the verge of the graveyard.

Her own territory, about three uneconomical acres of luxuriance and decay, was also bounded on all sides by the horizontal demands of agriculture, but there in the center of it, in the sun, a red-winged blackbird commanding the ruined windmill and insects shrilling in the lushness, Julia thought herself to be deep within a shaft of vital warmth. She had a canteen of water, a small lunch and a blanket in the car; it was Sunday afternoon, the memorial end of May, a day for rest. Rest she would, following the sun, the sun on her closed eyes, her mind for a time prescinded from its customary objects, but first she must pace through the remainder of the house, touch the windmill, look into the barn.

Downstairs the rooms were barren, save for an oak pump organ from which Julia squeezed a few sighing notes. Upstairs there was an attic with a water tank coated in pitch; below it were four plain bedrooms, a useless bathroom, bare electric bulbs without juice, dessicated flies on the windowsills. Julia looked out through wavy, dusty glass upon fields of sprouting corn and spring-green oats. A plain existence must have been had in this house, severely strictured in winter, briefly blowsed out in summer, much different in its rhythms from the farmhouse life she and Milton had improvised the first year of their marriage.

She had been teaching in a small town grade school. Milton had been writing his dissertation, alone during the day in the rented white frame house with the steamboat porch. He would be ready for her on her returns. Wait, she would laugh, wait, but there had been nothing to wait for: they had been alone, their beginning had been well-spoken and sealed; all around them fields of many colors had spread in concrete fecundity. Julia remembered cooking dinner afterwards in her bathrobe, moving back and forth within the loosened swell of her breasts, the delicious pout of her belly. Milton had grown a beard. She remembered his young forehead, the lids of his eyes as he sat reading, his body in the moonlight the July night they ran naked through the corn rows. So condensed that year and the intervening years seemed at this moment, as if she could press out all the confusions and fatigues and hold them essential and rounded in her hands! It was true: life was a breath; it was a single word blown into countless particles; it was a stupendous pot, containing everything, everything.

With her hand first on a wooden bannister and then on one of piping, she wound down two flights of stairs to the basement, where the once-whitewashed limestone walls now had made drifts of grey dust along the floor line. Julia touched cool stone. Down here darkness and light were sifted familiarly together. It was like other old basements she had been in, an atmospheric thickening and settling in which one could almost fancy lifting a fabled door and descending even further to an encounter. This floor, however, was crudely slathered with cement. There was a fruit cellar with rough shelving, a furnace room where a few lumps of coal remained in a corner, and in the center of the main room stood a washtub with a swivelling, squeaking wringer.

From an outside source came a wooden banging sound—a door? Had the wind come up? She looked up to a small ground-level window and saw unruffled grass interspersed with wild geranium, stilled bits of lavender among green, sunlight she could not feel. She turned slowly around in the enclosed air. "Milton? Milt?" she said aloud.

She climbed up into an emptiness of dust-filtered sunlight. Then, out in the barnyard, surrounded by a babel of insect and bird sounds, she heard dogs barking from down the road in Kaiser's direction and a metallic banging she knew to be the lids of pig troughs. A truck sped by, and in the distance was the toiling of a tractor. She saw no flapping doors.

The warmth was drawing a haze into the air. Julia shielded her eyes. Across the yard stood the sagging barn and closer to her on a slight knoll a shed and the broken windmill. She turned around. Yes, she had locked the kitchen door and put the key in her pocket. Turning, turning, she made a complete circle. To what place had she come? Now every part of her seemed to be listening. She was a woman sentient, whole, alone in grass, in sun, in a setting of decrepitude.

Well, she had to eat and drink; that much she knew.

She fetched her lunch from the car and spread the old plaid picnic blanket near the four metal feet of the windmill. This was the heart of the land. She was a visitor. She opened her food.

Nine-hundred-odd *souls* had read the population sign on the out-skirts of the town where she had been teaching when they were first married. Which total couldn't possibly have included them, they had joked, lovers uncounted, unassimilated into the community, burrowed in briefly between one census and the next. So perhaps that made them lost souls? they had surmised complacently to each other, secure as they were in the first hedonic flush of their union, where their primary task had been to become thoroughly imprinted, remade with love.

Julia stared at the crisscrossing of shadows cast by the doubled over windmill. What had become of them? They had moved to Milton's new job. The years had taken over. The world had taken over. Never again had they been able to pretend that they were separate from a community. In their own minds they had become like one small nexus within a vast web trembling upon the surface of the earth. Milton had thought it his duty feverishly to be receiving, organizing, answering pulsations from the world's network of brains; she had thought it hers scrupulously to be handing down the tools of language with which one received, organized, responded. They were parents, they told themselves; they were teachers; they were links between one generation and the next. The connections had seemed intelligible enough.

Finished now with her food, Julia got up to inspect the windmill. A huge wind it must have been, perhaps even a tornado, to have toppled those vanes. Here at the base of the tower was another pump, this one without a handle. Julia looked down. She was standing on a wooden trapdoor in the platform of the mill, a door with a large iron ring and mossy green in the cracks of the boards. She stepped aside, pulled the ring, and by wedging her foot in a crack of opening and grasping the edge of the door with both hands was able to heave it off to one side. A crumbling of earth fell down to the visible base of the hole with a deadened sound. There wasn't much to see—perhaps twelve feet of circular depth, a vertical well casing, a few horizontal pipes about six feet down. "Hoo-hoo," she called down into the coolness, "hoo-hoo," but there was scarcely any enlargement of her voice. Somewhere down there—at eighty feet? one hundred feet?—must be water.

"Come here," Milton would say to her late at night, in a voice thick with tiredness, "tell me some things, tell me a story."

Lying close, tired out herself, she would study his physiognomy. Time was lapsing. His career was waxing brilliant; his concentration pressed upon his chosen matter.

What had they chosen to speak about? Julia crouched at the edge of the well hole, meditatively dropping in bits of earth and grass. It would have been possible to say anything within the warm fragile orb of their intimacy. There had been two people, momentary quiet, the glow of a lamp.

Always, somewhere, then, as now, battles were being fought; in the night cries of children tore open the fears of parents; in the streets citizens did not trust each other; waves of illness would pass through the city; students and teachers alike struggled against stupefaction; both in and out of the marketplace rewards seldom seemed

commensurate with effort. Small private voices trembled like
flames.

Then, for Milton, the ultimate complication had set in. Time had
conclusively lapsed.

Julia tipped the trap door back into place and felt a slight shudder
in the earth. She stood above it in the hot sun, wiping her hands
upon her skirt. She was trembling, slightly dizzy from crouching
over. Might it have been possible for words to heal?

Whole cultures, so the tales went, could be lost in the lapse of
time. And individuals: could they be lost, could they be saved?

Death. The earthly web loosened. One fell. All the old connections were gone. This windmill shed, for instance, with its door
secured by rusty wire, its windows encrusted; this shed in whose
yellowish gloom she could make out wooden barrels and cobwebbed
pitch forks and tables of tools over which years of dirt had silted:
this shed was no longer a stopping place, no longer a holding place.
It was very easy.

Oh, she could feel how the loosening would come, the falling, the
losing, the slipping, the lapsing.

She wheeled around from the shed window: windmill, house,
barn, fields—all there—and back on the tower the red-winged
blackbird, calling kong-ka-ree, kong-ka-ree, against a hugeness of
sky.

Pink-flowered smartweed grew profusely in the barnyard, un-
trampled. Upon the few inches of dark water in the deep bottom of a
metal trough she could see the hazy blueness of sky, her own slip-
pery face at a far-away rim.

Julia first approached a side door of the barn, a double door
latched by two heavy iron hooks. At the limestone sill she stopped.
Ancient manure spread pockmarked before her into a dim interior
of stalls. She looked at the row of empty stalls a long time, as if trying to read them, and then she stepped back outside and latched
both doors.

Along the broad western side of the barn she made her way, stopping to peer into the cracks of missing boards and battens. Her body
cast its shadow, now upon a slit of interior, now up along the nearly
paintless exterior. She came to a large central wagon door where

enough lower boards were missing to allow her to creep inside.

Straightening up, she beheld a vast, two-story space, an alley-way striped confusingly with sunlight, lined with doorways, some closed, some darkly missing, crudely laddered here and there to the lofts.

From the emptiness came sounds, animal, with breaths. In the lofty, sky-patched dimness a small bird flew from one rafter to another. Slowly Julia moved forward across bars of light, across dusty leavings of hay. The sounds, perhaps human, drew her on, past views of slanted wooden hay racks, more stalls, rows of barrels, unpartitioned rooms with straw-covered floors where direct light here and there was turning straw into gold.

What are you making? Julia had asked Sally once when the four-year-old had been sitting on the kitchen floor, intently turning an egg beater. "I spinning gold into straw," Sally had answered. Julia had loved and often repeated that story of a child's blithe reversal, in which the spinner and the spinning had been more valuable than either gold or straw.

The last doorless opening on the right gave her the origin of the sound, which she must have sensed all along, for she felt no surprise, rather a deep recognition: a boy and girl on a blanket of blue, the primordial, flexuous two-backed animal that lives however it can: here at this moment in a borrowed corner already so seasoned by ruttishness that one more instance seemed merely to sink anonymously into it, as bodies sink, are absorbed into gravity.

Then Julia saw the eyes of the girl, and the eyes of the girl focused upon her, only for a second before Julia turned away, but long enough for the individual embodiment of all yearning to be recalled to her, no matter how many thousands of tongues had formed it before.

She emerged from the barn into the full western sun, into a resurgence of wind, a fleece of airborne water swiftly approaching from the southwest. It was now simply a matter of gathering up her things and going home—she knew that—of going forward like a wheel turning upon its navel. Ground appeared to be covered; trees, fences, hedgerows marched in order on either side. The church door was opened by Minnie in an apron, its strapless bib pinned to her dress, who accepted the key, asked no questions, proffered a pint of honey for which she would take no money.

Julia stood on the doorway slab with the jar of viscous gold in her hands. "I'll come back with a loaf of my bread sometime."

Minnie nodded her wizened head. "You do come back," she said. "Come back on your bicycle. Minnie liked that." She opened her partly toothless mouth and laughed with soundless mirth.

Christopher was waiting for Julia on the broad front porch in the old wooden lounge chair. The lawn with its scattering of trees sloped greenly down to the street. It was nearly June. Gathering clouds now covered the sun. All day he had been basking in the exhilaration of his success. He had wakened late, relaxed, had breakfasted long on his terrace, had taken his turns through the city park and along the river, all the while contemplating this delectable world where pieces could be made to come together, where patience and vision finally yielded a whole. It was immensely satisfying.

Christopher thought about the powerful heat of the sun, just beyond the clouds. His agile mind was working now upon an article he had been reading that morning. The future was in the sun; the solar panels in this current project were just a beginning for him. From now on he must systematically put his money towards the sun. He needed more young people around him. He thought magnanimously of his nephews and neices. He felt himself to be rich, instrumental, forward-looking. He folded his hands on his chest and thought warmly about the future.

But where was Julia? The telephone had been ringing behind the locked door. He had expected to come up the driveway and surprise her as she worked in the flower beds. He had wanted to pluck her up and coax her out for an evening. He had in mind a ceremony, of the sort Julia herself had always been such a genius at concocting, for tonight a low-key, decent commemoration between them of this extraordinary season of loss and regeneration. He saw himself pouring out wine and saying something of this sort, raising his glass to dear Julia in this extraordinary season of loss and regeneration. Or should he say *renewal? transfiguration?* A bit giddy with his own well-being, he raised his empty hand to the sky. Should he say, I drink to the sun in this extraordinary season?

He slept. The sun dropped clear of a rim of clouds and buttered the lawn and the leaves of the pin oak, the sweet gum, the linden. Tendrils of clematis vine swayed from the porch trellis, their delicate curls of shadow, unseen by Christopher, floating upon the white clapboards. His mind and body were being laved by the state of consciousness called sleep. It is said we are born not knowing that which we are. It is said we can be taught. Here. On this earth.

He looked so peaceful that Julia was careful not to wake him. She lay supine against the cushions of the porch swing and with a dangling hand slowly rocked herself in place. Here they were again, she thought, she and he, this old friend from childhood, like cattle back in their stalls in the evening hour. How do you fare, brother? And you, sister, how do you fare?

Milton was not here. There was no way now to lie close, breath beside breath, to say, tell me something, to ask, husband, how fare you?

She rocked herself with the tip of a finger. It was the end of this particular day. It was time for rest.

The ringing of the telephone woke them abruptly. "Stay," said Julia, "I'll answer it."

How strange the living room looked at this moment, as if she were a visitor in her own house!

"John, is that you? I'm so glad to hear your voice. Speak up, will you?" Julia sat down beside the telephone, holding a handful of blouse together at her throat. "What's that?" she asked. "I don't think I'm hearing you properly."

"But how can you think of that, Johnny? You have no idea. All right, all right, I'll just listen."

She listened to her son. She tried to picture him as he was now, the size of him, the way his beard grew, but instead she saw him as an infant in his crib, sleeping with his knees tucked under him, his head perfect, downy.

She listened to a voice that seemed about to crack in its suppressed excitement. Johnny was attempting mightily to sound calm, organized, mature. The girl, Julia supposed, might even be in his room, might be sitting on his lap. She tried to remember this girl. She took a comb out of her hair and began to rake up the wisps along the back of her neck.

"What do you think your father would say?" she asked. "At least come home to talk about it."

"Well, I'm sorry, I'm too surprised. My sense of timing is shaken up. What about your examinations?"

"I'm glad to hear that. Listen, John, do come home for a talk."

"Of course bring her if you want."

Julia had been making sweeping marks in the carpet with her bare toes, making marks and then erasing them and then making them again.

"Yes, that's fine," she said, "I'll be done teaching by the end of next week. I'm not going anywhere."

After the call she sat still by the telephone, staring across the room at the fireplace. It was never done with, she thought, this being torn open by your children. It was useless to say that they were not still connected, that the cord had been cut; for her it had simply grown longer, more tenuous, its vibrations exquisitely deeper.

At last she pushed herself up, got a drink of water in the kitchen and then went back to the front porch. Christopher was winding his pocket watch.

"Johnny says he wants to get married," she announced as she returned to the swing.

"Married."

"Yes, married."

"Who is the mother of the child?"

"Christopher! He says there is no baby, and the girl is Cynthia, the one I met when I visited him last fall."

Christopher sighed. They both were silent. Julia pushed the swing with her foot.

"What time is it?" she asked finally.

"Almost seven. I was hoping to take you out to dinner tonight."

"Dinner?" She looked at him and then down at herself. "Christopher, I can't. I don't have the energy to wash my feet."

"I'll wash them for you."

"You're absurd. You're sweet. Thank you, but I'm not hungry. I just want to have some milk and go to bed."

"That's not enough."

"Of course it is. You're just like Father. You think that life will stop if you don't get your three meals. On time. Aren't you ever sick to your stomach?''

"Never," said Christopher. "I take big chances with business; with food, never."

"You're lucky you've always had enough to eat."

"So are you."

"Well," said Julia, giving the swing an extra push, "I don't think I'll cook anything tonight."

Brother and sister faced straight ahead, contemplating the lawn. There was a moist greenness now to the atmosphere, a low, intermittent sun, heavy clouds.

"It will rain before long," remarked Julia.

"When is this wonderful wedding to be?"

"They say that out of consideration for their parents, they have decided to wait until July."

"Out of consideration, in July," repeated Christopher.

"There never was such a one for dreaming as Johnny. And for stubbornness. Christopher, what can I say to him?"

"Wait and see what her parents say. There are worse things in the world than getting married."

She looked at him acutely. "Would you care to be quoted on that?"

"I don't set myself up as an example, Julia. I'm not particularly proud of the way I've lived."

"Of course you are. You're particularly proud of never having depended on anyone, particularly a woman."

"You're a woman. I've gotten a lot from you."

"That's not the same. I came ready-made."

"Here, here." He moved to the swing and sat beside her. "What sort of talk is this?" He took one of her hands in both of his. He was surprised at its warmth. He was surprised at the ache in his own heart. "You're not ready-made," he said, "and neither am I."

"Christopher, I'm so worried about Johnny."

"Of course you are."

"Milton would turn over."

"It will work out. Everything works out in time."

"No, it doesn't!" cried Julia. "Don't you see? I'm afraid he'll be lost."

"How can he be lost? He's still Johnny. There are all sorts of ways to live."

She looked at him. Her eyes went back and forth over his familiar face. She saw his broad forehead, his white hair, the high coloring they had both inherited from their mother, the tendency toward jowls that came from their father, the blue gaze.

Her own eyes felt as if they were connected to the earnest center of her heart. "Christopher," she said, "we must speak to him. He is still so very young."

"Of course we'll speak to him." He put an arm around her, and she leaned back her head. "I will speak to him most particularly about the financial aspects."

"He has no idea," said Julia. "Oh, why can't they just live together?"

Christopher laughed. "Well, let's find out what his ideas are. That's the first step. And remember: you can only lead a horse to water."

"That's what I don't understand. If we are all so connected, why does there still seem only just so much we can do for each other? I *watched* Milton die—don't you see?—and I did not know what to say."

"What could you have said?"

"Something that would save him, I don't know."

"No," said Christopher, "it was his life. You were patient. You didn't run away from what was happening."

His words were easing a knot of grief in her. She rolled her head gratefully back and forth across his arm. "How did you come to sound so wise?" she asked.

"Listening to you all these years."

"I'm the one listening to you."

"Then will you please come to dinner with me now?"

She looked him full in the face: her brother. She smiled. "You go get your food. I'm going to do exactly as I said. I'm going to have some milk and get some sleep for my fifth graders."

He smiled in return. "You talk like that, and then you wonder where your children get their stubbornness."

"Christopher, this has been the most astounding year."

"You're coming through all right. I've been keeping half an eye on you."

"I know you have. I've felt it." Her body relaxed into the motions of the swing. The connections, she thought, were all still there, only perhaps a thousand times more mysterious than she had accounted for. "Thank you, Christopher," she said.

She did not turn on the lamps. In a house permeable to the approaching night, to the approaching rain, she undressed and bathed and put on a nightgown she had had for twenty years. Her hair, as she bent over to brush it, fell forward in a coarse, white mass. Bare feet, faded garment, arms, hands, hair: this was her body, her vehicle, her merest shelter; this was the remnant of a marriage.

"Dear God," she said aloud.

She lay down in the middle of the bed and watched the windows, where now and then one of the puffing curtains would catch for a moment on the back of the rocking chair. When the rain began about nine o'clock, she got up once more to check through the house.

Thunder and lightning opened up the night; driving rain sluiced through it. The noise and flashings were too tremendous to allow sleep. Julia stretched out on the bedroom carpet, with a view of the active, night-green pine tree outside, and began to exercise. Her legs were getting stronger, she could tell, and she could turn her head more easily, without as much constriction in her shoulders. It felt good to twist and bend and roll, to feel blood moving, to lie back in a tingling restfulness.

Voices of the storm became quieter. She was lying so still it was as if the rain were washing through her, rain coming in due season, a natural eulogy.

For a moment she becomes nothing but a channel for this sweetness, this water, this love.

That night she dreams that she is following a deep cut in the earth, such as might be found on an archaeological site. There is a bank of clay on the left of the earthen path and on the right a sharp dropping off. Unafraid, she rushes along, sure-footed, until she stops before a huge, primitive face crudely carved high relief into the clay bank, features prominent and angular. From every orifice—eyes, nose, mouth, ears—come tongues of flame as well as growing branches of leaves. Red and green. There is a low rushing sound, like the wind of a fire. Julia looks and looks and then she is riding her bicycle down the paths and around the curving hedges of a labyrinthian formal garden. It is summer. She is balanced on her bicycle, and she is also high above the maze, watching a white-haired woman passing fluently beside the hedges. She is looking for Milton. She is looking for Johnny. She thinks all her family must be somewhere in this garden. She pedals around a green bend. She is listening for the origin of a double musical sound she hears, high and low at once, like a single voice that has divided into two tones and now sings both together.